Caledonian Cabal

Almek Manning Book 3

By J.A. Dalley

This is a work of J.A. Dalley
http://www.almekmanning.com
Copyright © 2014 by James Andrew Dalley

Cover Art by Graphicz X Designs

ISBN: 978-0-9858049-4-7
PRINTED IN THE UNITED STATES
First Printing: June 2014

To All the military personnel
Who have died in the service of their country

PRAISE FOR THE ZOCHTIL

"We have aliens from both sides of the fence. What I mean by this is that we don't have aliens that are all against us, and we don't have aliens that are all for us, and in some cases we have aliens that are more or less neutral…

"The characters in this book are very well-formed, you feel an attachment to each one of them, and when one of them fails or is killed you feel the sadness with or for them. In addition to well formed characters the storyline was well written, I found it quite exciting, and I enjoyed the fast-paced action scenes, as well as some of the more average training in day-to-day activities scenes."

~Matt McIntosh
SciFiFX.com

"As a big fan of science fiction I found The Zochtil to be a great story and an enjoyable read. The depth of the characters and the pace of the story keeps the reader engrossed and wanting to know what happens next. Packed with action and plenty of sci-fi elements, J.A. Dalley creates a universe that draws you in and makes you feel as if you are right there with the characters. The Zochtil is the first book in the series and I for one can't wait to read the next books to come."

~James Freeland
Author of *Star Catcher*

Chapter 1
Changes in the Crew

"She can't take it anymore, Captain!" Commander Duval yelled over the intercom. "I recommend we give the order to abandon ship, sir."

Captain Haldeman only took three seconds to make his decision, but the pain was evident on his face. "Understood," he said. "Boatswain's mate, sound the call to abandon ship."

The boatswain blew his pipe, then said, "All hands abandon ship! All hands abandon ship!"

"Get out of here, Captain," Lieutenant Stock, the general quarters officer-of-the-deck urged.

"The captain goes down with his ship," Haldeman said, without a trace of hesitation in his voice.

"Not today, sir. I'm not leaving, so either we both go down or you leave."

The captain locked his gaze with Lieutenant Stock for a few short seconds, and then Captain Haldeman nodded.

"You win. I've enjoyed having you under my command," Haldeman said, as he hurried to an escape pod.

"Let's hold her together for as long as possible," Commander Duval told Lieutenant Stock.

"Will do, ma'am."

Commander Duval died at her post when engineering took a direct hit from a Draconian penetrator missile. Lieutenant Stock died a few seconds later when a plasma beam shot a blast through the hull of the *Heinlein*, and the bridge was breached. They were both posthumously promoted to the rank of captain and were both awarded the Dalton Space Force Medal of Honor.

I saw a flash, and I relived the deaths of other friends. Kate, Spencer, Alan, Ryan, and Collin, had all died when we tried to escape from London Proper. Many more had died in the Battle of the Blockade. Still more had died on the colony station Plymouth as it took a direct hit from a Monarch-class battleship.

"Captain," the voice of my executive officer, Jennifer Kade, snapped me awake in a cold sweat.

"Yes, X?" I replied. I was still a little shaky from the nightmare, but I was already halfway into my uniform.

"Sir, someone is here to meet you. They're in the hangar."

"Say again?" I asked. The *Starwarden* was cruising just above light speed toward Lexington, one of Jack Dalton's colonies outside of Sol System. We had jumped into the system going at low Kelven speeds. Our Kelven drive wasn't operating quite up to spec since the beating we took at the Battle for the Orbitals. We were still a light day away from Lexington, and no one should have been meeting us until we reached orbit.

"Someone is here to meet you, sir. She says that she has secure information from the Sky Marshal and Jack Dalton. She's in the hangar."

"How?" I asked. "No fighter or shuttle can go at K-speeds."

"Apparently this one can," Jenny said. "Kai is already headed to the hangar to admire the craft."

"I'm sure he is. I'm on my way."

I decided to grab my dress jacket and donned it over my ship suit. I passed by a couple Canids, dog-like humanoids who were one of our best allies. Unfortunately, there weren't many of them left. The Draconians had tried to eliminate all of them, but their ruler, High Alpha Sonnel, managed to escape with a crew of a couple hundred and had sought refuge in Sol System.

"Captain." I turned to see who had called out to me.

"Yes, Lieutenant Grumak?" I asked the Passerine.

Passerines were very odd-looking people. They had elfin features, pointed ears, youthful faces, and wings, but they stood an average of seven and a half feet tall, with their wings easily adding a foot to their height. It was sometimes hard to retain command presence in front of someone who looked like an angel and towered above humans.

"How long are we going to be here at Lexington, sir?"

"The current plan is a week, why?"

"Well, I think I've worked out some of the problems with the K-drive. Richard is eager to test them."

"I'm sure he is," I said, smiling. Commander Richard Winters was my engineering officer. However, his skills were wasted serving on a ship. He had worked for both Solar Fleet R&D and The Lab. He loved working on a ship, but we needed him back at The Lab where he could develop new toys for us to play with in the battlefield.

"I'll talk with you later, Grumak," I said, as I reached the hangar. "I have some business to attend to."

I arrived in the hangar just in time to see the pilot getting out of the cockpit of a fighter that looked like a cross between a Spaceraider and a Tomcat. When the pilot jumped down to the deck, I was shocked to see how short he was. I was accustomed to working with a human crew on the taller end of the spectrum and Passerines who towered over humans. And this pilot couldn't have been an inch over five feet.

When she took off her helmet, revealing long locks of red hair and brilliant hazel eyes, I was surprised and a bit confused. Few crewwomen or officers have long hair. Hair just gets in the way if the ship loses gravity, and no aviator has long hair, since it is even more impractical in a fighter.

"Captain Manning, I assume," the short aviator said.

"Yes, and you are?"

"Captain Shey Hunter, quad-ace, and holder of three naval crosses and not less then seven medals for distinguished flying. I'm your new CAG."

"The commander of my space group is Kai Drove," I said,

thinking there was obviously a mix-up. Kai Drove was the best pilot in the Force, and I couldn't afford to lose him.

"Not anymore, sir. Kai is relieved of command effective immediately."

"What?" Kai asked as he picked the most inopportune time to dash into the hangar.

"Excuse me," I said. I was losing patience with this stuck-up aviator. "*I* am the Captain here."

"I have my orders."

"And I give those orders, if you are, in fact, under my command."

She handed me a memory orb. "All the information you need is stored on this. Most of your officers are being replaced."

"Captain, what's going on?" Kai asked.

I was really lost, but I knew I needed to see what was on this orb. "Captain Hunter, stay here with your spacecraft. I'll be back. Kai, I'm not sure. Just keep an eye on her."

"As you say, sir."

I went through a side door and into the aviators' briefing room. I locked the door behind me and plugged the orb into the console. I navigated through the files until I found what I was looking for.

"Almek," the face of Jack Dalton said, as the recording started up. "You have some of the best people in the Four Species Alliance aboard your ship. Many of them are needed elsewhere. Richard Winters has been reassigned to The Lab. I need Kai to report to the flight school over Colony One. Captain Hunter is at least up to par with Kai if not better, but she isn't worth a dust storm on Mars as a teacher. Commander Jennifer Kade has been promoted to Captain, and she has a ship to command. Commander Kyle Kern is going to be the exec of Captain Kade's ship. There are many other transfers that also need to be made. The Sky Marshal waited to send these instructions to you until you reached Lexington, because he didn't want to deal with your arguments. You are to release all of your transferred crew to the cruiser *Prideful* when she arrives in system, which should be around the same time that you achieve orbit over Lexington. Good luck."

I called the Sky Marshal a couple of choice words under my breath. Sometimes the Sky Marshal, commander of both the Solar Fleet and the Solar Marine Corps, got on my nerves. He had good reason to give me these orders when I was out of range for a secure communication link. When he assigned my girlfriend to an EMP grapeshot frigate a few months ago, I just about jumped down his throat, because I knew the casualty rate of grapeshot frigates was unbearably high.

I settled deeper into the chair. The *Starwarden* was a new construction. She had only been commissioned eight months ago. She'd had the same crew the whole time. Now I would be losing the top echelon of human officers. All my Canid and Passerine officers would stay aboard, but I would only be keeping Lieutenant Commander Jade Robins, who just happened to be the best navigator in the Alliance, and Lieutenant Emily Connaley, my comm officer and human chaplain.

It wasn't good to change up the officers like that. On the other hand, I wasn't very likely to convince the Sky Marshal to countermand his orders. If I wasn't worried that the United Monarchy of Europe might be able to intercept our communication link, I would have opened a channel with the Sky Marshal anyway.

I opened up an implant link with all of my officers. *This is Captain Almek Manning. All human officers report to the wardroom immediately. I know it will be a tight squeeze, but we must meet face to face. All Passerine and Canid officers may view the broadcast from the secondary wardroom.*

I walked out into the hangar and found Shey showing off her custom fighter to Kai. I knew that Kai was tense after hearing that Shey was my new CAG, but that didn't stop him from admiring a good fighter.

"Come with me, Commander," I told her.

"Sir?"

There is only ever one captain on a naval warship, and that is the skipper of the ship, *the* Captain. Normally, other captains are bumped up one rank socially. For example, Captain Kai Drove, my former CAG was always called commodore, but if the Captain wishes he can bump a captain in his chain of command a rank downward and call her commander. I didn't like this snotty aviator, so she would be Commander Hunter until she proved herself worthy of being called anything else.

We walked through a few corridors before we bumped into Commander Chandler, my supply officer.

"Suppo," I called out. "Can you assign Commander Hunter a temporary bunk?"

"Sure thing, Captain," he said. "Come with me, commander, and I'll get you settled in."

"So will you tell me what's up now?" Kai asked.

"You're being transferred, along with most of *Starwarden*'s officers."

"What ... why?"

"It's what Dalton and the Sky Marshal think is best. I won't contest it. I'm not happy about it, but it *will* happen."

"Yes, sir."

I reached the wardroom just as Commander Kade ... Captain Kade arrived.

"Captain," she nodded at me.

"Commodore," I replied.

She glanced at me sharply. "What did you say, Almek?"

I handed her an orb that contained her orders and the specs of the ship she would be commanding. She plugged it into her palm reader and gasped.

"But I belong here," she said, looking at me pleadingly.

"If we weren't at war, I would agree," I said. "But we are. You are *easily* captain material."

"Sir," she objected. "I've always been your second-in-command. I'm not leaving you."

I love Jenny. She and I had a lot of history together back in the London Proper Detention Facility. She had saved my life many times, and now we thought of each other as brother and sister. It was going to be hard for both of us, but there was a war on. Plus, I wanted to organize a rescue mission to save our friends who were still in London Proper. If I was going to get the Sky Marshal to approve that plan I'd need to stay on his good side.

"What class will you be commanding?" I asked, ignoring her statement.

"Sir, don't make me leave. You can contest this."

"Jen," I said, putting a hand on her shoulder. "I'm going to miss you more than you know, but you *are* captain quality. The Alliance needs you to be commanding a warship, not helping me command one. My new XO won't be as good as you, but I'll survive."

"Almek," Jenny started to say.

"No. You're taking the ship. What class?" I asked again.

She glanced down at her datapad again. "I'll be among the first ten captains of the Solar Fleet's fast-cruiser carriers."

"*Heinlein*-class?"

"Yes, sir."

"They're among the best."

"That they are, sir," Jenny said, a faint smile coming to her face.

We waited in silence while the rest of the officers arrived. Commander Ardent, my Canid XO, and Commander Drumair, my Passerine XO, arrived shortly after Jenny did, and I gave them the quick rundown of the situation.

"Men and women of the *Starwarden*," I said, once all the officers had arrived. "It has been my great pleasure to serve with you for these past months. All of you have provided great service while on this ship. And, together, we earned the Presidential

Council's Unit Citation with a Silver Star. However, we are at war with no less than three enemies. We cannot sit back and relax while our enemies grow stronger. We must continue to fight.

"The Sky Marshal and Jack Dalton have given almost every human officer aboard this ship new orders. Ten of you are getting your own command. Another twenty will be getting first officer slots, and most of the rest of you will be at least department heads. Once we reach the orbit of Lexington, we will be met by the *Prideful*. She will bring the new officers to the *Starwarden*, and our departing officers will transfer to the *Prideful*.

"I expect you to show the rest of the Alliance how great it was to serve on this ship. Uphold the honor of being a valued member of the *Starwarden* family, serve to the best of your abilities on your new ships, and fight for the everlasting glory of the Alliance. Good luck!"

"Dismissed," Jenny called out. "I will be contacting each of you within the hour with your new orders."

***

The next day I was saying goodbye to my officers as they boarded the *Prideful*.

"Jenny," I said, giving her a hug and holding tight.

"Almek, I don't think it's very proper for the captain of a ship to hug his first officer," Jenny said, hugging back and trying not to cry.

"It isn't like anyone's going to court martial me for that," I said.

Jenny laughed, and we broke our hug.

"We've been through a lot together," she said. "From London Proper to captains of two great warships, the *Starwarden* and the *H. Beam Piper*."

"It has been great, hasn't it?" I agreed.

"Yeah, it has. Don't worry. I expect to be on your staff when you're promoted to Sky Marshal."

I laughed. "Okay. If I ever have a command that gives me an opportunity to pull you back, I'll do it."

"You'd better."

"Jenny," I said, as she was turning around. "I almost forgot." I handed her a memory orb.

"What's this?" she asked.

"It's my proposal on how to spring our friends out of London Proper. Please make sure this gets to the Sky Marshal."

"I will," Jenny said. "This is just as important to me. I don't know when I'll see him, but as soon as I get a change, I'll give this to him."

"Thanks."

It was going to be hard running my ship without Jenny at my side. She had been my second-in-command when we were in London Proper. She had always been a sure voice of reason on my team. I had relied on Jenny while in London Proper. The Sky Marshal had broken that reliance when he sent me to be the Solar Fleet liaison with Dalton Space Force. I had been put in a command position without Jenny at my side, and I adapted. However, once I was given the *Starwarden*, Jenny had easily slid back into her role as my second-in-command, my executive officer. I knew that she would make a great captain, but it wasn't going to be easy for me to be a great captain without her. I had worked with other executive officers at Boot Camp, like Isaac Jones, but I had never clicked with anyone like I had with Jenny.

"Richard," I said, turning to him, as Jenny boarded the *Prideful*.

"Yes, Captain."

"I want you to come up with some new toys for me to play with."

He smiled from ear to ear. "I have some ideas, but I've been so busy getting this ship back together that there hasn't been any time. Just make sure your new engineer, Lieutenant Commander Duval, doesn't do too much damage to *my* engineering spaces."

"I'll try, and if he does, I'll make sure to call you."

"You do that," Richard said with a smile. "See you later, Almek."

Richard boarded the ship, and the hatch closed behind him. It was going to be an interesting couple of months getting this new batch of officers into battle readiness. Especially Commander Shey Hunter. However, I looked forward to talking with Lieutenant Commander Duval. I hoped he could match his mother's engineering ability. I had served under her on the *RAH*, and she had been a great engineer.

I went up to my stateroom, so that I could look over the records of my new officers. I started out with the most junior ensigns and worked my way up the list. I had only just finished with the ensigns when my implant was pinged by the Master Chief Webb. Chefo was the man in charge of all the meals, and every member of the crew loved him. He could make anything taste great, and he was also able to cook meals that the Canids and Passerines said were brilliant.

Yeah, Chefo? I asked.

It's half an hour after your usual mealtime. Are you planning to have dinner tonight?

I checked the clock on my implant and, sure enough, Chefo was right. *I got caught up with work. Could you bring me whatever it was you cooked today?*

Sure thing, Skipper. I'll be there in a couple seconds.

I moved onto the lieutenant junior grades, while waiting for Chefo to show up. He arrived shortly, carrying a tray weighed down with food.

"Can I help you with anything else, sir?" Chefo asked, putting the tray on my table.

"Yeah," I said, looking down at the food. "Help me eat it."

Chefo laughed. "I thought you'd be up late. So, I gave you extra food for later on tonight."

"Chefo, what would I do without you?"

"Starve, or at least forget to eat for a couple days."

"Probably," I said, smiling at him.

"I've got work to get back to, sir. The new supply officer wants to inspect the galley tonight."

"Chefo," I called out before he could exit. "I need to talk with you."

"Fire when ready, sir," he said, turning around at the hatch.

"Everyone in the crew likes you, and you always seem to know everything about everybody on the ship."

"I try to stay connected so I can be useful, sir."

"How do the enlisted feel about the change in officers?" I asked him.

"This could take a bit," Chefo said. "May I sit down, sir?"

"Yes, please." I gestured toward the empty chair.

"Thanks. I don't like what the Sky Marshal and Mr. Dalton did. It may be good from a Fleet perspective, but it really, and I do mean *really* hurt crew morale. You were never enlisted, but you were a JO right?"

"Yes, of course. Not long enough, in my opinion, but I was an ensign and a lieutenant."

"Well, you have to learn just how to work with each officer. Some like you to do a task one way, while others want you to do the same task a different way."

"Yeah." I nodded my understanding.

"If you change out one to five officers at a time that doesn't make a huge impact on the ship. Some things have to change, but stability is maintained. However, we've got a completely new officer cadre. The ship is going to change drastically, and a lot of crew members are going to get chewed out for doing something the right way under their previous officers, but doing it in a way that their current officers don't like."

"I see what you mean, Chefo. Is there anything I can do to help?"

"I've thought about this for quite awhile, sir. That is, I thought about it the whole time I was making lunch and dinner. The only thing I was able to come up with would be to promote a couple of the enlisted. For example, Chief Petty Officer Kristine Taggart. I know she doesn't want to be an officer, but she would make a great ACICO. She can run CIC like no one else. Except maybe you, Captain."

"She can run it much better than I can. I don't think she would accept the promotion, though. She doesn't want to be an officer."

"I know that, sir. But this is war. We need all the officers we can get. We need good enlisted too, but Kris has command presence. If she becomes an officer she would be commanding a warship within a couple of years."

"I agree. I'll think about what you said, Chefo. Thanks a lot. I'll instruct our new suppo to give you an extra day for the inspection. Dismissed."

"Thank you, sir!"

I did think about it, and, before I had even touched my food, I called Kris Taggart to my stateroom.

"Chief Petty Officer Kristine Taggart reporting as ordered, sir."

"Drop the salute, Kris. Sit down."

"Thank you, sir."

"Kris, how's crew morale right now?" I asked her.

"Bad, sir. These new officers are not making people happy. My CIC crew has already been chewed out multiple times."

"That problem was brought to my attention. What if I told you I had a solution to ease the tension in CIC."

"I'd love to hear it, sir."

"I'm promoting you."

"Sir," Kris said. "I would love the promotion, but what difference does it make if I'm a senior chief instead of a chief?"

"None."

"Then what are you saying, sir?" Kris was now confused.

"I'm promoting you to ensign, Kris."

"I don't have the education, and you can't do that to me, sir!" Kris said, jumping up from her chair and knocking it to the deck. She picked it up, but the fire in her eyes wasn't abated by the mishap.

"I can, Kris. I need an ACICO. That *will* be you."

"Sir," Kris said. "I don't want to be an officer. I like where I am now."

"Kris," I said, looking directly in her eyes. "I would much rather be an ensign right now, but I'm a captain. I took on extra responsibility because of the war. Now I'm asking you to do the same."

Kris was silent for a long time as she stared off into space.

She sighed heavily, and we locked gazes again. "I'll do it, sir, but I can't say I like it."

"That's fine. I'll swear you in now. I expect you to move into officer quarters tonight. Your duties as ACICO start tomorrow."

"Understood, sir."

Chapter 2
Commander Shey Hunter

The next day, I had breakfast in my stateroom while pouring over the records of my lieutenant commanders. I got tired of those and moved on to the record of my biggest problem, Captain Shey Hunter. Though she had an amazing combat record, her record outside of combat was far short of pleasant. She had been hauled up for captain's mast, or non-judicial punishment, twice. NJP was common for enlisted personnel, but officers were more likely to get thrown out of the service through a court martial than to go through NJP. However, if you went to NJP multiple times as an officer, that was really odd. It was almost the weirdest form of a compliment, while still being a reprimand. It said that Shey had significantly messed up multiple times, but was so valuable that we couldn't afford to throw her out. She was obviously a good pilot, but could she become a good leader? I wondered just why Jack Dalton had replaced Kai with Shey…

I was jerked out of my thoughts when a message flashed in front of my eyes. I had an incoming link request from the planetary governor.

Opening link, I said formally.

Captain Manning, the governor began, clearly upset. *There is a spacecraft flying around my tugs and constructors and disrupting the work on our orbitals. She claims to belong to your ship.*

I swore under my breath before I responded. *Let me contact her. I believe she does. Please hold….* I quickly opened up a link with Shey. She rejected it. I growled at her, while I opened up a function I didn't like using. I punched my link through. As CO I could do this, but I'd never had to do it before.

Shey Hunter!

Yes, sir.

What the hell are you doing out there?

Practicing, sir.

If you want to practice, you can use the flight sims.

They aren't like the real thing.

Commander Hunter, I said, trying to remain civil. *You <u>will</u> return to the ship now! You are grounded until further notice. And I won't hesitate to haul you up for a court martial if you disobey a direct order.*

Sir, I'm just …

I swore at her in English, then Canid. *Get back here <u>now</u>!*

She didn't respond, so I pulled up the scanners on my holodisplay. I saw her lone fighter heading back to the ship.

Governor, I said, returning to his link. *I am sorry, and I <u>will</u> deal with this problem.*

Thank you. Ending link.

"Bridge, this is the Captain."

"Captain, bridge," I couldn't recognize the voice.

"Who is standing watch as OOD?" I asked.

"Lieutenant Ball, sir."

"Who gave permission for the flight drill?" I asked.

"Sir?" Lieutenant Ball said. "According to standing orders, the CAG has the responsibility for arranging those. She told me that she was running one."

"Sorry," I said. "You're right, Lieutenant."

I closed the channel, running my fingers through my hair. I had forgotten for a moment that the young idiot hotshot that was showboating around civ spacecraft was the CAG of my space wing.

I rushed to the hangar, calling up the Master-at-Arms along the way.

Sheriff, I said, once he opened the link.

Yes, sir.

I'm in need of your services in the hangar.

Yes, sir. I'll be there in ten seconds.

Sure enough, I got there and found Master-at-Arms William Tobias already waiting at the hatch. I saw that he had a stunner strapped to his leg. I nodded approvingly, and we both entered the hangar. We got there just as the spacecraft came in through the mass driver, and I watched in awe as the fighter that had been going close to half-light was slowed down to less than forty klicks. The fighter hit the reverse thrusters and landed smoothly. Shey taxied into her slot and climbed out.

"Commander Hunter, you are relieved of command and grounded, until further notice. You are not to be anywhere near the hangar or the aviators' briefing room. Do you understand?" I asked.

"Sir, I would…"

"The captain asked you a question," MA Tobias said, as his hand drifted down to his stunner.

"Sir, yes, sir!" she spat out.

"Good," I said. "The Master-at-Arms will escort you to your quarters. Do not disobey my orders."

I went up to the bridge and was pleased to see Emily on duty.

"Emily," I said. "I know we can't guarantee a secure link, but I *must* talk with Mr. Dalton now."

"I'll do the best I can," she said.

I waited for five minutes, before she had me take her seat. I pressed a button, and the sound enclosure field enveloped me.

"Jack," I said.

"What is it?" he asked. "You know this isn't secure."

"It's Captain Hunter," I said, ignoring his statement.

I heard Jack sigh heavily on his end. "What has she done now?"

I explained the issue and waited for his comments.

"Almek," he began after a long pause. "Shey has been nothing but trouble for me since the hostilities with the Draconians came to a standstill. She is the best pilot in the Force during battle, but she's hopeless outside of a dogfight. I was hoping you could cure her."

"Jack," I replied after another long pause. "I was almost starting to think we were friends, and then you pull a stunt like the Sky Marshal would pull."

I could almost see Jack smiling. "Sorry, Almek."

"Thanks a lot."

I closed the channel and got up, heading for my stateroom. *Commander Dale*, I said opening up a link with her. *I would like to see you in my stateroom. I need to brief you.*

Commander Jessica Dale was waiting at the hatch to my stateroom when I got there.

"Commander." I nodded at her. "Come on in."

I sat down at my desk, and Jessica took the empty chair. I saw her glance toward my 'I Love Me Wall.' 'I Love Me Wall' is unofficial military jargon for the wall where an officer places all of the memorabilia from his or her previous duty posts or commands.

I glanced over at it myself. Hanging there, I had my diploma from the Academy, and my medals from DSF and the Solar Fleet. I also had a picture of Big Bertha drawn by one of the spacemen who had served on her during the first battle of the First Interstellar War. It was signed by all of Big Bertha's surviving crewmembers, and, at the bottom, it read, "In Memory of Captain Rockwell." Next to that was the blueprint of the *Robert Anson Heinlein*. I had purchased that from Jack after I was transferred to the *Starwarden*. The *RAH* was my first ship, and it would always have a special place in my heart. In the center of the wall was something the crew of the *Heinlein* had given me when I was promoted to Captain and was given command of the Colony One orbitals. It was a three-dimensional holographic representation, in full color, of the UES *Mayflower*.

"What do you think?" I asked her.

"Very impressive."

For the first time since she had arrived, I really looked at my new executive officer. She appeared to be in her thirties, probably thirty-five. She was wearing the standard blue ship suit that all personnel on the *Starwarden* wore, but she had Dalton Space Force insignia on her left shoulder. She was a little on the short side. I was sure she would be intimidated by the Passerines who towered over her. Her black hair was cut short in the standard spacer fashion.

"What's your 'Love Me Wall' like?" I asked her.

"Not that impressive. I've been with DSI since it started accepting applications for military recruitment. I passed the tests and got put on the officer track. From there, I started out as an ensign in security. I was still an ensign when DSF built its first ship, and I served on her. By the time the war started, I was a Lieutenant. I was in the first skirmish above Colony One and then was promoted to Lieutenant Commander. I've served on the *John Paul Jones* since then. I was just recently promoted to Commander, and here I am," she said matter-of-factly.

"Well, things on this ship are very different from any other," I began.

"I'm sure that's an understatement," she said.

"Yes, it is. You know I have three executive officers. According to standing orders, you outrank the other two executive officers."

"Okay," she acknowledged.

"I did that originally because Jenny had always been my right hand. I hope you can continue that."

"I'll try, sir."

"That's another thing," I said. "Jenny only called me sir on the bridge and on duty. In my stateroom, call me Captain or Almek. Not sir."

"Got it, Almek," she said.

"May I call you Jessica?"

"Yes, of course."

"Okay, Jessica. Both Ardent and Drumair report to their respective species' military leader. You, however, only report to me. You do not report to either Jack Dalton or the Sky Marshal."

"I understand."

"Are you going to have any issues working directly with

aliens?" I asked her.

"No, sir. I'm not xenophobic."

"Everyone says that," I replied. "Then they start working with aliens. Things can change. I've had to send a handful of human crewmen back to replacement depot, because they couldn't handle it."

"Don't worry, Almek. You won't be sending me to repple-depple."

"Good. For the next two weeks, we are going to eat breakfast here in my stateroom. I want to know you better, and you need to know me better if you're to be my right hand."

"Sounds good."

"Okay, dismissed."

She got up and opened the hatch.

"Jessica."

"Yeah, Almek?"

"Go to Commander Shey Hunter's quarters. Tell her she is free to move about the ship and that her flight status has been reinstated. Also, tell her I will adjust standing orders so that no flight drills are preformed without my say-so."

"Will do."

I was going to like my new executive officer. She wasn't Jenny by any stretch of the imagination, but she was going to be a good officer and, hopefully, a good friend, too.

Chapter 3
Adjustments

I had known this transition would be rough. Chefo and Kris had confirmed my opinion, but I would never have guessed how bad things would eventually become.

I had designated Tuesdays as "complaint day". This meant that any off-duty officer or enlisted could come to my cabin and discuss any issue with me. This was an unusual practice, but I was in command of an unusual ship. I always left my schedule open and usually reserved Tuesdays for catching up on my paperwork. With my original crew, I had received maybe ten complaints a week, and most of them were easy and relatively trivial to deal with. The first complaint day with my new cadre of officers was four days after the transfer, and, when Jessica left my stateroom after our breakfast together, I was shocked to see a long line of crew, both human and alien stretching down the corridor and around the first bend.

"I think you may have more than you bargained for, Captain," Jessica commented.

"I think so," I said. "Can you tell Ardent and Drumair that I may need their help, along with yours, at some point today."

"I'll pass that information along," Jessica said.

"One other thing. Get Tobias down here fast."

"Aye, aye."

I then turned to face my first crewmember. "Come on in," I said and gestured to the seat that Jessica had just vacated.

"Thank you, sir."

I closed the hatch and sat down, too, "What's the issue Chief?"

And so began a very long day. Most of the issues were easy to handle. It was just my enlisted complaining about getting chewed out. I didn't like it, but I wasn't sure what to do about it. Tobias kept the crew orderly and helped with crowd control. A minor scuffle broke out between two crewmembers, and Tobias had to take them down to the brig to cool off. I hated seeing my crew so messed up.

After I took a quick seven-minute lunch break–at the insistence of Chefo–I was just about ready to stop fielding complaints for the day, but I felt I needed to talk with at least one more person.

Tobias opened my hatch, and a Canid came in. There were very few Canids aboard, because there were very few Canids left anywhere in the galaxy, and each one aboard was valuable and highly skilled.

"How may I help you, Senior Chief Serd?"

"Sir, I am here to report xenophobic harassment."

Ardent, I need you here stat! Then I spoke to the Canid. "What happened?"

"One of your new engineers, Lieutenant JG Datlow, chewed me out for the way I was handling antimatter, which I did by the book, sir, I swear. After he chewed me out, he said, and I quote 'No dumb dog should be allowed to handle dangerous materials.'"

At that point Tobias opened the hatch for Commander Ardent, my Canid XO.

"What is your specialty?" I asked Serd.

"Antimatter drives, sir."

"Ardent, is Senior Chief Serd good at his job?"

"Among the best, sir."

"I *will* rectify this problem right now," I told Serd. "Ardent come with me."

We both headed out of the stateroom, with Tobias in tow, after I assured everyone else I would come back. It didn't take long to locate Datlow.

"Lieutenant," I addressed the engineer. "I do not tolerate xenophobic harassment on my ship. You will be taken to the marine base on Lexington, and there you will be held until a court martial can be convened."

"What is this about? Did the Canid squeal?"

"Canids don't squeal," Ardent said, a low growl building in his throat.

"Tobias take him to the hangar."

"Yes, sir."

There weren't any other major complaints that day, but Chefo visited me again that night.

"Captain," he said, rapping on the hatch

"Come in, Chefo."

"Sir, I have an issue with your new CAG."

"What did Shey do this time?" I asked.

"She apparently has a food allergy that I was not informed of and was unable to eat what I prepared for the officers. She stormed past the Chief I keep near the door to dissuade people from entering the galley and headed straight for me. She informed me of her allergy and said I needed to fix her something edible. I told her that I was sorry, but I had been unaware of her allergy. I offered to make her a sandwich, since I had already cleaned up the galley and was preparing for an inspection. She said she didn't want a sandwich and expected me to make her food just like everyone else. I told her I would see what I could do and came straight to you."

"This is nowhere near my first issue with this officer," I told Chefo. "Make her a nice sandwich and have her report to me if she doesn't like the sandwich."

"Will do, sir."

***

I met with all my new officers the next day in the officer's wardroom.

"I'm sure that you all know about the disaster of a complaint day I had yesterday." I saw many nods among the officers. "Let me tell you this: if you were all to die right now, and then a Draconian Wrym-class battleship were to jump into this system, my crew would be able to destroy it. However, if you were to lead my crew in battle against that same Wrym-class battleship, we would most certainly die."

I watched the faces of my officers. Most were shocked, though some of them did understand.

"I'm not saying that you are bad officers, nor that you're not as combat savvy as the crew, but I am saying that you are not part of my crew yet. The *Starwarden* is unlike any ship in the Alliance. So are her crewmembers. I want all of you to have a meeting with the leading chief in your department. Ask him or her how things are done in your section. If you want to make any changes to how things have been done, I want you to talk them over with your leading chief. I know this is unorthodox, but the *Starwarden* is unorthodox. Get used to it. I don't want to deal with a line of complaints that long ever again. If I do, we will be having a much longer meeting next Wednesday. If you have any problems, come to me directly. We are at war, and the flagship of the Alliance can't afford to be this messed up. Is this understood?"

"Yes, sir," I heard almost everyone say.

"Good, dismissed."

After all of the officers had cleared out, I noticed that Kris was still seated and waiting for me.

"What's up, Kris?" I asked her.

"I don't like this whole officer thing," Kris said. "I miss my old friends, they all call me 'ma'am' now."

"That's life, Kris. Weren't you the one who explained this same issue to *me* at Boot Camp way back when?"

Kris smiled. "I did, sir."

"Come on, you can still be friendly with them, but this is war. I need you as an ensign."

"I understand, sir. It isn't easy, though."

"Nothing in the mil is easy, Kris."

"Touché," she said and got up. "Thanks, Captain."

"Anytime, Kris."

Captain, Jessica said as I opened the link.

What is it?

Shey's gotten into trouble again, sir.

Part 1
Monarch-Class Battleships

Chapter 4

The Long-Range Tornado

Things aboard the *Starwarden* improved rapidly after that meeting. Besides Shey Hunter being a constant pain in the rear, life returned more or less to normal. However, there was still a war going on, and, three months after the transfer, I was in a meeting with the Big Three–The Sky Marshal, Jack Dalton, and High Admiral Numair–plotting and planning.

"Do we have any options yet?" Sky Marshal Bartholomew Kitt asked Richard Winters.

"Sir," he said, "I know about as much about the phasing technology as I do about the Garm, which means I only know what the Passerines have told us."

"Numair?" Kitt said, turning to face the holographic projection of the Passerine military leader.

"I swear I've given you all we know about them. The Passerines have almost no knowledge of the Ancient Ones. We've been in space for many centuries. But we've also been through so much warfare that our records aren't the best. We have the specs of a shield device that can force ships to remain in our dimension, but you already know that. Their weapons are far stronger than anything even the Garm have, but they stopped attacking us suddenly, and we don't know why."

"All I know," Richard said, turning the conversation back to the real issue, "is that these ships phase out, for a mater of seconds. This allows them to avoid our strongest weapons, including our antimatter torpedoes. I need a way to test different types of torpedoes against this phasing drive, but I can't do any testing other than with highly inaccurate sims. I need a working phase drive."

"Zarc ambassador," Jack requested, "do you have any information that your mighty people would grace us with?" Jack's voice dripped with sarcasm, but it wasn't something the Zarc seemed to understand.

The shapeless cloud that was all we were permitted to see of the Zarc did nothing for a long while, and then it finally spoke up. "All I am allowed to say at this time is that we know of these Ancient Ones. The best earth name we could give them is Phobians."

"Like the moon of Mars?" I asked.

"Yes, that is the planet they once occupied," the cloud said. "They were a powerful militaristic race."

"Are you saying they're Martians?" the Sky Marshal asked.

"No race ever inhabited that planet before you. The Phobians didn't even have an outpost on Mars."

"What happened to them?"

"We eliminated them," the cloud stated coolly.

I shook my head in confusion. "I thought you abhorred violence."

"We do, but the destruction of these creatures was necessary. I may not speak further of this."

It was nearly impossible to read the emotions of the Zarc, but I would have been willing to bet my bottom credit that the Zarc ambassador was quite upset. He seemed to have told us too much about these Phobians.

"Do you think the UME may have reverse-engineered technology from Phobian relics?" Jack asked.

"My people believed they had eliminated all traces of the Phobians from this galaxy. It appears we were inaccurate."

The ambassador seemed content with that sentence. We waited a while longer, but he wouldn't elaborate.

"Can you tell us more?" I asked him. "What sort of technology could the UME have gotten their hands on?"

"We will only know once they use it," the cloud stated.

"Can't you give us hints about their other weaponry?" Richard asked.

"No," the Zarc said. "You may be able to use their ideas to create stronger weapons. That is not within the scope of our treaty."

"If your race failed to eliminate all traces of the Phobians, don't your people have an obligation to clean up the unfinished business?"

"The Zarc are no longer a part of this galaxy. We are only helping because our government is currently under control of a party that believes in assisting those who are less developed. However, the military is not governed by that party."

I was tremendously interested by his comments. The Zarc had never revealed so much about their people or government in the past year as this ambassador had in the past few minutes. I could practically hear the wheels in Richard's brain spinning as he tried to interpret all of this new information.

However, despite further questioning by the Big Three, the Zarc ambassador wouldn't say another word. He had gone mute, as had happened so many times before.

"Well," Jack said, turning back to Richard. "What can we do without the help of the Zarc?"

"There isn't much we can do," Richard said. "As I already stated, I need a working phase drive to run tests on. I've been back at the Lab three months now, and I've done all I can without an actual drive."

"So, all we have to do to please you is capture an intact Monarch-class battleship?" the Sky Marshal asked.

"I'm sure that our Joint Spec Ops teams could pull that off," Richard said, referring to the combined STAR, Blue Squadron, Force Recon, and Wingman teams we had used to capture two Draconian ships.

"Even our spec ops teams can't infiltrate a Monarch-class while it's on the ground," the Sky Marshal said. "And I'm not ready to authorize an all-out attack when we can't guarantee our weapons will even be able to hit the enemy ships."

"I'll continue my research," Richard said. "But I can't make any promises without solid intel."

"I'll work on that," the Sky Marshal promised.

"Then I believe this meeting is over," Jack said, standing up. "Thank you all for attending."

"Sky Marshal," I said, walking up to him after the meeting was over. "Did Jenny give you my proposal?"

"Yes," he said, not making eye contact. "We can't risk a ground assault."

"We have to do it. I promised my men I'd go back for them."

"I didn't," the Sky Marshal stated flatly.

"Jack," I said, turning to him.

"I have my ideas and I *will* discuss this with you," he said. "But now is not the time."

I pressed him to know when would be the right time, but he was no more helpful than the Zarc ambassador.

After giving up on learning anything from Jack, I ran to catch up with Richard.

"Rich, how ya doin'?"

"I preferred being *Starwarden's* engineering officer over heading up The Lab," he said, with a faint smile. "I can't figure out what to do about the phasing drive. I simply don't have enough data."

"You can do it, buddy," I said, patting him on the shoulder. "Jack absolutely knew what he was doing when he pulled you back to The Lab."

"Thanks," he said, but he didn't look convinced.

"Look, Richard," I said, stopping him and turning him to face me. "We can make it through this, and you can solve this problem. We all have your back. Don't worry."

"Thanks again." He pulled out his pad and walked down the hall.

***

"Captain, bridge," Jade said over my comm channel a couple weeks later.

"Bridge, this is the captain. What's up?"

"We've got a Long-Range Tornado on our screens, sir. I'd like you on the bridge."

"On my way."

I was already halfway to the lift before Jade had requested my presence on the bridge. Thanks to my standing orders not to shout attention while under general quarters, I was able to enter the bridge with only a brief acknowledgement from the Boatswain's Mate.

"Captain's on the bridge."

I took my seat and pulled up the sensors. Sure enough, there was a Long-Range Tornado just three hundred klicks away.

"Are there any others?" I asked Jade.

"No, sir."

"Just what is a Tornado doing this close to Colony One?"

The *Starwarden* was back on her patrol of human territory. We did a slow circuit from Earth to Lexington to Colony One. It seemed that, once again, a small fighter had intercepted us part way to our destination.

I hadn't expected an answer, but since the Captain had asked, someone answered.

"Sir, it may have been tracking us."

"Thank you, ensign. I'll consider that. Send out a tug with a five spacecraft escort, Jade."

"Wilco."

Shey, I commed her. *This is your first chance to prove yourself. You haven't left me with a favorable impression yet. If you want to keep your job, just remember you're acting under my orders on this mission.*

Yes, sir.

"Sir," a watchstander cried out. "The Tornado just lit up like a

Christmas tree."

"What do you mean, Travers?" Jade asked.

"All of her systems just went hot. Weapons could be charging."

"Is there anything a lone Tornado could do against the *Starwarden*?" Jade asked

"Not by conventional means, ma'am," the BM said. I could clearly hear the comment he left unsaid: we don't know what alien tech they may have.

Jade nodded. "CIC, bridge. Any guesses?"

"Bridge, CIC. No clue."

"I've got an incoming transmission, sir." Emily said.

"Transfer to my screen," I ordered. I looked at the small holodisplay on my chair arm.

"This is Elizabeth Kendrick. Come in *Starwarden*."

Elizabeth Kendrick had been one of my squad members in London Proper. Why in the world would she be in a Tornado? Had she escaped? Or was this a clever deception?

"All fighters," I said, opening a channel. "Do *not* fire on the Tornado. I repeat do *not* fire on the Tornado." I closed that channel and opened up a new one with the Tornado. "This is Captain Almek Manning. Elizabeth it's good to hear you."

"Squad Lead," I could hear the smile in her voice. "You have no idea how great it is to hear you again."

"Elizabeth, I want to believe it's you, but I'm not sure I can."

"I understand that," she said. "I'll stay way outside self-destruct danger zone, and transmit a vid message to you."

"Okay, I'll have my comm officer grab it. Stay put. I'll have someone pick you up." I transferred the circuit to Emily, then turned to Jade. "Jade, order one of the runabouts made ready."

"I'll get the first lieutenant on it immediately, sir."

"X," I linked up with my three executive officers. "I need you guys in my stateroom."

***

"And that's our situation," I told them after I'd explained it to them. "I would like to believe her, but how would she have gotten hold of a Long-Range Tornado?"

Ardent smiled at me for a second before speaking. "And this coming from the man who escaped London Proper by hijacking a hovercraft."

I chuckled, remembering that time so long ago when I had commanded a gang of teenagers, and we had raided a UME naval base. "True, but a Long-Range Tornado? Our intel says that those are kept under top security. And we aren't even factoring in her ability to fly one all the way out here to Colony One or track me down."

"Why don't we withhold judgment until we review the message?" Drumair asked.

"Good idea." I said. I opened up a link with Emily. "Emily, do you have the vid?"

"I've got it on an orb, and I'm headed down right now."

We waited in silence, each doing our own work, while we waited for Emily.

"Here you are, sir," Emily said, handing over the orb.

"Let's see what's up," I said, plugging the orb into the holoprojector in my table.

The face of another old friend from London Proper appeared. It was the face of George McCloud. He was a proud Irishman, and his family had been part of an organization whose goal was to liberate Ireland from the UME so it could join the Presidential Council. I had tried many times to make him an officer in my squad, but he had always refused the post.

"Almek, I would address you by your title, but the reports I'm receiving indicate your rank keeps changing. I hope you'll recognize me. I have lots to tell you about London Proper to convince you of the reality of my situation, but I must offer you a proposition first.

"I'm a Captain in the UME Marine Corps, but I'm not happy with the UME. There are many others who do not believe in the UME. We've formed an underground. I didn't start it, but I now have close to fifty under my command in this cabal.

"I'm currently stationed on Mars, and I can offer you a brand new Monarch-class battleship if you are willing to help me. I have no way of knowing for sure if you can help me, but I will proceed with the plan that I am about to outline in the hope that you are in a position to help.

"In one month, on the fifth of May, my men will capture the Monarch-class battleship currently named *Marx*. I have two members of the underground in place aboard the ship as officers. They will be able to collect all of the command codes needed to conn the ship. The underground does not need help getting the ship into space, but we will need help escaping beyond Mars orbit. At the end of this message is all the information the underground has assembled about the Martian orbital defenses and about the UME ships in the vicinity of Mars. As I said, we'll need help to get the Monarch away from Mars."

This was just what Richard had wanted. If George McCloud could really deliver a Monarch, that would put us in striking range of defeating the UME. But could we trust him, or was this just a clever plot to destroy more Solar Fleet ships.

"Now that I've made my proposition, I'll tell you the story of London Proper…"

"Pause the recording," I ordered. *Commodore Hunter, I need you to bring the Tornado aboard as soon as possible, preferably by yesterday.* "Jade, I want us to be back in L-5 orbit around Dalton Spaceways in forty-five minutes. Emily, I need you to contact the Big Three. Tell them to all be at a secure room on Dalton Spaceways in an hour. I don't care what they say. Let them know that this trumps any other priorities. We have a lot of planning to do."

"All hands prepare for jump. We will be going FTL in five minutes. All hands ..." the BM of the watch called out.

"Resume playback," I instructed.

Chapter 5
The Tale of London Proper

"Over the fence!" Kathy shouted. "They're right on our six!"

She watched as her squad slowly climbed over the fence.

"Move it, people!" She looked around and saw the two Wolverine helicopters headed toward her group. She gave one last instruction to her troops and then climbed over the fence herself.

"Everyone get to cover!" one of her lieutenants said.

As soon as the teenagers had reached the London Proper side of the fence, they scattered. Not all of them made it over, though. The Wolverines spat out a blast of electricity and the fence lit up like a fireworks display. The seven people still on the fence were all killed.

"RTB, guys," Kathy told them once the Wolverines left the area.

"I hope Almek gets back soon," one of Almek's squad members said.

"He'll come back as soon as possible," Kathy said.

***

Barely two weeks had passed when two Wolverines appeared in the sky again. They prowled the city for hours. One of them started to burn down the crops that Kathy had just inherited from Almek's squad.

"Let's show them who's boss here," Kathy said. "Grab one of our RPGs, McCloud. Let's take these guys down."

McCloud returned quickly with an RPG launcher. Kathy loaded it up, put it on her shoulder and tracked the Wolverine. She waited until she had a solid lock on the enemy helo, then fired. She didn't even look to see if it hit. She instantly started loading it up and focused on the second Wolverine, which was swooping in to see what had happened. She didn't wait for a lock this time. She tracked the helo and kissed the missile on its way. It collided neatly with its target.

"McCloud," Kathy ordered. "Get a fireteam rounded up, and check out the first helo. I've got the second one."

No one was alive, but Kathy and McCloud were able to salvage quite a bit of extra equipment from the helos. The best thing they retrieved was a Vulcan cannon with lots of ammo. Kathy assigned her techie to set it up on the roof of their base.

"More will come," she explained to him. "I need that working by tonight."

"I'll try."

"That is unacceptable," she said. "It's tonight or you're out of the squad."

"Understood."

"The correct response is 'Aye, aye, ma'am'," George McCloud said. "We seem to be at war. You guys need to pick up the military structure that Almek had maintained in our squad."

Kathy nodded thoughtfully. "I believe you're right, McCloud. Spread the word. You're a commander now."

"Ma'am?"

"Don't argue, Commander."

"Aye, aye, ma'am," he said, grinning.

***

Kathy was right. That night five more Wolverines came in. They shot at anything that moved. Kathy's squad was able to take down all five Wolverines with no losses to her squad, though many others in London Proper were killed. However, they were down to only three rocket-propelled grenades, and they had used up half of the ammo for the Vulcan. They salvaged another Vulcan and more ammo from the downed helos and set up the second Vulcan.

The Wolverines came again the next night, but the people of

London Proper didn't have a chance. Ten Tornados streaked across the sky, dropping canisters of gas. Kathy had been prepared for such an attack. Half of her squad had gas masks, and the others were deep underground.

"Here come the troop carriers," McCloud said through his mask.

"I see them," Kathy said. "All forces, hold your fire. They won't expect anyone to be conscious. Let's wait until they make themselves good targets."

The troop carriers fired more canisters of gas around the city before they started circling for a landing.

"Now!" Kathy shouted over the radio.

Both Vulcan cannons started up, and the remaining three RPGs were fired into the hearts of three helos. Ten troop carriers and five Wolverines were taken down before they ran out of ammo.

"Time to move underground," Kathy said. "Let's go."

She led her team to the system of underground tunnels they had discovered many years ago. They appeared to have once been maglev stations or a more primitive mode of travel. The signs simply labeled them as "underground" stations.

"Remember," Kathy said. "We fight for our freedom!"

Kathy and her squad fought a fierce guerrilla war for three months, hitting the UME, stealing supplies, and then running for cover. But the casualty rate was high. Squad members would go on watch or patrol and never be seen again. Finally, the UME Force Recon team snuck in one night, and all the remaining squad members were taken prisoner while they slept. They awoke in a holding cell.

"Which one of you is the leader?" a fierce looking man with sergeant stripes asked.

No one said anything. Kathy wasn't around. She had been on watch that night.

"You've killed them all," McCloud retorted. "Our last officer was standing watch tonight."

"Not a surprise," the sergeant said. "This was too easy. I don't know how any of you managed to escape in the first place."

He must have had an odd definition of easy, McCloud thought. We killed hundreds of them.

"The rest of you are, as of this moment, conscripted into the United Monarchy of Europe's Marine Corps. Perform and you'll live. Mess up and you're dead."

***

"The next year was a year of hell," George McCloud continued to explain. "Kathy's squad had been a little under sixty strong after she had absorbed your squad, Almek. After three months of war, the squad was down to fourteen who were captured. The sergeant killed four the first day. Of the remaining ten, only four of us survived boot camp. It wasn't that we hadn't endured worse, but the instructors had it in for us. We were shot rather than getting lashes, being thrown in the brig, or even being assigned extra duty.

"Out of the four who survived boot camp, only two of us are left: that would be Elizabeth and me."

"Pause," I said. "Everyone leave," I ordered.

Once my three execs and Emily had left, I laid down my head and cried. I had promised that I would come back to save them. Instead they had all died. I had been naive not to realize the UME would retaliate against London Proper. I should have taken the entire squad. If only I had realized the obvious.

You can't dwell on the 'what ifs,' Annabeth's soothing voice said.

"Annabeth?" I asked out loud, before I realized she had been talking to me via implant. *Annabeth*, I said again.

Yeah. You opened up a link to me again.

I seem to do that a lot. Annabeth had been my girlfriend back when we lived in London Proper. I wouldn't have been able to withstand the rigors of leading a gang of teenagers struggling for their lives without her there at my side. Once we had escaped the Presidential Council territory and joined the Fleet, we had parted ways. She had joined the Judge Advocate General's Corps to become a Fleet Lawyer, and I had gone into the Academy and had become a captain. However, I still relied on her comfort in the years since we had separated. I loved Lauren with all my heart, but Annabeth was a shoulder I could lean on so easily.

Annabeth. I just found out that our squad was wiped out by the UME.

I know, she said.

How?

We have satellites, she said in exasperation. *The Sky Marshal has known for a long time that London Proper was raided.*

I felt like screaming at the Sky Marshal.

Almek, calm down. There was nothing we could do about it. The place was crawling with UME Marines, and the SMC wasn't in a position to do anything about it. Our squad died fighting. They always knew that was a risk.

Why didn't you tell me?

I didn't have the heart to break the news to you.

You didn't have the right to hold back something like that! They were my soldiers! I had the right to know.

Fine, Annabeth said. *I was ordered not to tell you. The Sky Marshal has been leading you on. He didn't want you to know.*

But it's my fault.

Yes, Almek it is. I was surprised at her harsh statement. *But what have you done since you got back? And how many people have died in those battles?*

But ...

Almek, no buts. Get over it. I understand your pain. I share your pain. You gave them your word that you would come back for them when you were able. They were all killed long before there was even a chance. The battle started while we were still fighting for our lives in a court martial.

But ...

Almek, it's brutal. The losses are unacceptable, but there's nothing we can do now but accept them.

Ending link, I spat.

I knew that Annabeth was right, but I felt so guilty that I hadn't tried harder and sooner. After another few minutes, I brought the execs back in, and we finished the recording.

"I can provide little other proof. I do not need assistance getting the *Marx* off the ground. I just need ships in space above Mars ready to protect us. Once again, I will continue as planned. I hope to see you in a month. If you have any questions, Elizabeth Kendrick should be able to answer most of them. Major George McCloud out."

The message ended.

"Captain Manning, Bridge."

"Bridge, this is Captain Manning."

"We have docked with Dalton Spaceways, sir."

"Captain, this is Emily."

"Go ahead, Emily."

"Needless to say, the Sky Marshal, Jack Dalton, Sonnel, and High Admiral Numair are anxious to learn why *you* have ordered *them* to be waiting. You have five minutes to get to the secure room. I suggest you book it."

"Thanks, Emily," I said. "Okay, let's go. Drumair, you stay here with the ship."

Normally, I would have left Jenny behind and would have brought Drumair with me, but I wanted my new exec, Jessica, to gain some experience dealing with the Big Three.

We booked it to the secure room. Under usual circumstances a captain would not be seen running frantically through the halls of Dalton Spaceways, but one doesn't order around the Big Three and then arrive late to the meeting. I arrived exactly on time.

Chapter 6
G2

"Captain Almek Manning reporting as ordered," I said, saluting the brass in the room.

The Sky Marshal raised his eyebrows at me, while Jack burst into laughter.

"Reporting as ordered?" he asked, after his laughter subsided. "Didn't you order yourself here?"

"Yes, sir, but I figured it wouldn't hurt to be polite."

"Let's just get to why *you* ordered *us* here," the Sky Marshal said.

I wanted to exchange some choice words with the Sky Marshal, but that wasn't going to win me any points right now. So I outlined how we were tracked down by Elizabeth Kendrick and recounted her story. Then I set up the holoprojector, and we watched George McCloud tell his story.

***

"You believe that this is George McCloud?" Jack asked.

"I do, sir."

"You believe that he is telling the truth?" the Sky Marshal asked.

"McCloud is one of the best soldiers I had in London Proper. If it is McCloud, which I believe it is, then he would never be a willing participant in a UME-inspired plot. His family was part of a civilian underground operating in UME territory. They were captured, and McCloud was sent to London Proper after they killed his parents. He hates the UME."

"I would like to speak to this Elizabeth Kendrick," Sonnel said.

Sheriff.

Yes, sir.

Escort Kendrick to the secure room.

Wilco.

"She is on the way," I told them.

As soon as MA Tobias accompanied her to our meeting room, the Sky Marshal and Dalton started grilling her with questions about UME boot camp and her UME career. Then they asked her about how she had escaped with a Tornado.

"The underground arranged it," she said. "They made sure this mission had no connection to McCloud besides McCloud's historic connection to me. I was serving on Titan. The cabal has almost fifty percent of the officers on Titan."

"Just how large is this cabal?" Jack Dalton asked, leaning forward and resting his elbows on the table.

"Compared to the size of the UME military, we are very small. However, we have a four-star general and a three-star admiral in the cabal. We have been slowly gathering people on Titan, and Major McCloud has more than enough people on Mars to take the *Marx*."

"Does the cabal have a name?" I asked.

"G2."

"G2?" the Sky Marshal asked. "That's standard jargon for intel."

"G2 was also the Irish intelligence group, like the historic CIA or MI6 organizations. However, when the UME took over, G2 went underground. Most of the Irish didn't like losing their freedom again. The Scottish were also proud of the freedom they had gained at the end of the third world war. They formed a united organization, though they each use their own name. The Irish call it G2, and the Scottish call it the Caledonian Cabal."

"And do you honestly think that McCloud can steal a Monarch-class battleship?" Jack asked.

"He will either steal it or blow the ship up. There is no other option," Kendrick said.

"Why have you contacted us now?" the Sky Marshal asked.

"That's a little more complicated," Kendrick said. "G2 has

wanted to make contact long before this, but they were unsure if you would believe them."

"I was contacted three or four years ago," Jack said. "But, at that point, I just gave them the standard response that DSI was a neutral organization. I promised I wouldn't reveal their organization, nor would I help it."

"And you didn't mention it before?" the Sky Marshal asked.

"I assumed they had been caught long before we ever had an official alliance."

"We were not," Kendrick said. "The G2 leadership thought that, because of our close friendship with Captain Manning, we might actually convince you to help us. Especially if we could include a Monarch-class battleship in the deal. We've been planning this mission since we learned of Almek's promotion to command the *Starwarden*."

"So, Almek was your highest-ranking point of contact with the Alliance?" Jack asked.

"Exactly. We had failed before to make our case with you, and we hoped that our connection with Almek would change the game," Kendrick said. "Otherwise, we figured we would have no meaningful chance to convince you to be there, ready to help McCloud, on the 5th."

"Do you have any other intel on the UME?" the Sky Marshal asked.

"Yes," Kendrick replied. "The G2 leadership gave me a couple orbs to pass on to you." She reached into her pocket and pulled out two orbs.

She handed one orb to the Sky Marshal and one to Jack Dalton. The Sky Marshal plugged his orb into his tablet, while Jack put his orb in his watch. They scanned the data for a few minutes.

"This is invaluable," the Sky Marshal soberly observed.

"And confirms our worst fears," Jack Dalton said, looking up with horror in his eyes. "They've gathered a lot of alien tech."

Jack took his watch off and handed it to the High Admiral.

"This does appear to be the technology of the Ancient Enemy. We must show this to our Zarc ambassador and see if it interests him."

"Do that," Jack said, "but, first, let me duplicate it." He took the other orb from the Sky Marshal and pushed them into slots in the table. Two orbs popped out, and he handed them to Numair while repeating the process again and giving two to the Sky Marshal and keeping two for himself. "We'll be in contact. Elizabeth, for now, you will stay on the *Starwarden* with Almek. We *will* act on this intel. Thank you."

"You're welcome," she said.

In a rush of movement, the leaders of the Alliance were gone. I had wanted to confront the Sky Marshal about London Proper, but he obviously didn't want to talk about it, so I escorted Elizabeth back to the ship.

***

"What should we do with our guest?" I asked my executive officers.

"She should be confined to her quarters," Commander Dale replied. "We don't know for sure that she isn't a spy."

I wanted to object, but I held my tongue until all of my execs had voiced their opinion.

"I believe that she is not a danger to the ship, but she is not an asset to the crew either," Ardent said. "We should have Master-at-Arms Tobias assign someone to her, so that she always has an escort, just to make sure she doesn't get into trouble."

"I agree with Ardent," Drumair said.

"As do I," I said. "Commander Dale, please inform MA Tobias of his new assignment."

"Yes, sir."

I headed down to engineering to talk with Lieutenant Commander Duval.

"Commander," I called out once I entered the engineering spaces.

"Yes, Captain?"

"How's the ship?"

"Sir," he said. "The ship is in good working order."

"Is she ready to head into battle alone against a couple of monarchs?" I asked.

"Sir?" Duval asked. He seemed to be trying to gauge my seriousness.

"I'm dead serious, Duval. Is our cloaking device online yet? I know it wasn't scheduled to be tested for another two months. I need it ready in three weeks."

"Sir?" he repeated with a note of resistance in his voice. I decided he needed some executive encouragement, though not in front of his men.

"Alex," I said, calling him by his first name. "Let's talk about this in private."

Once we were situated in a nearby briefing room, I bluntly tackled the schedule.

"Alex," I said. "You're on the Four Species Alliance Ship *Starwarden*. We do crazy things on this ship, and we do them at a minute's notice."

"Yes, sir," he nodded.

"Part of being chief engineer is dealing with impossible requests. This particular crazy request can't be retracted, but I need you to be completely honest with me about when this can actually get done and what resources you need. Understood?"

"Yes, sir."

"Okay, I need to know if the cloaking device can be up in three weeks."

"Sir, I would have to reschedule everything else not absolutely vital to the operation of the ship, but I should be able to run the first test in two weeks. If all goes well it's possible we could have it up in three, but I'll have to assign double shifts for my entire staff for the next three weeks to have a chance of succeeding. If the test doesn't go well we'll need to meet again."

"Is engineering ready for battle?"

"Yes, sir. All battle systems are functioning at eighty to ninety percent efficiency."

"Good," I said, standing up and slapping him on the shoulder. "And welcome to *Starwarden's* engineering."

"Thank you, sir."

***

The next day, I found myself, once again, in a meeting with the Big Three.

"We have decided to trust Kendrick, McCloud, and the cabal," Jack told me. "And, of course, your ship is going to lead this op."

"Of course," I said, nodding at him. "Who else?"

"You will also be supported by the Joint Spec Ops boarding shuttles," the Sky Marshal responded. "The shuttles won't be able to go in your hangar though. They'll attach to your hull."

"Will I have shuttles from all five teams?"

"Yes," Numair said.

"Will your ship's cloaking device be ready by then?" the Sky Marshal asked.

"I just talked to engineering about that yesterday," I replied. "We'll run the first test in thirteen days, and the device will be operational by zero hour."

"Good," Jack said. "We'll also double your complement of fighters for this mission."

"Sir, while my space wing was under the command of Captain Drove, I would have welcomed more fighters. But, right now, my wing is barely functioning as a unit. I can't afford to double them."

"So, I take it things with Shey aren't going too well?" Jack asked.

"Not at all, sir."

"Okay, we won't double your fighter squadron."

"So this is how the op will go down," the Sky Marshal said, plugging an orb into the central holodisplay. "The UME always has five monarchs, with smaller escorts, in orbit over Mars. McCloud will bring the *Marx* off of Mars from here." I watched as the *Marx* rose from the surface. The enemy monarchs started to fire on them. Then I watched as the *Starwarden* appeared in a slightly higher orbit. "You will drop your cloak as soon as the *Marx* is fired upon. Then you deliver everything you have from your ship."

"I've got The Lab working with the Passerines on making a holding field projector," Jack said, interrupting the Sky Marshal. "We hope to be able to give you one for this mission."

"Anyway," the Sky Marshal continued. "The *Marx* needs to get to this point." A point slightly above the *Starwarden* lit up. "From there, he can engage his K-drive, and the two of you will book it to Colony One. I would like to send a couple Jones-class carriers with you, but they'll just slow you down. The *Zochtil* will be standing by with a small fleet, ready to open up a wormhole, but that is only if the *Starwarden* is in danger. If we have to leave the *Marx* we will. We will not endanger our flagship any more than necessary."

"I understand," I said.

"Good, dismissed."

I stood up, saluted, and left. This was going to be a fun mission.

***

The next two weeks were hectic for the engineering crew. Lieutenant Commander Duval sent me daily updates, and everyone in the engineering crew knew that if we didn't get our cloaking device online, we would lose our opportunity to grab the most valuable UME intel yet: an intact monarch.

However, engineering wasn't my only problem. I had to take care of a couple Captain's Mast cases. Even a good ship has a Captain's Mast every once in awhile. Sailors will be sailors. Normally, the number of mast cases was kept to a minimum by only allowing a few personnel ashore at a time, but while engineering was going through such major revisions, we kept an airlock permanently open to Dalton Spaceways. So, we naturally had a couple of bar fights and a few drunk and disorderly charges that I had to deal with under NJP. Once I finished those cases, I had two more serious cases.

Lieutenant Commander Duval walked in with Master at Arms Tobias not far behind, leading a spaceman in handcuffs.

"There had better be a good explanation as to why I haven't heard about this already," I said.

"This is a very recent development, sir," Duval said.

"What happened?"

"Sir, you remember me reporting Spaceman Pickett being AWOL for three days, right?"

"I remember that, Commander."

"This is the spaceman. We found him..."

"Don't I get a turn?" the spaceman interrupted.

"Only if you wait until called upon," I said. "Things look pretty bad for you so far, so don't push it."

The spaceman shut up without directly acknowledging my statement.

"Anyway," Duval began again, "we, that is to say the Port MPs, found this spaceman involved in some highly illegal activities just this morning. He was turned over to MA Tobias just thirty minutes ago."

"So, who would like to tell me about these highly illegal activities?" I asked the group at large. "Would you like to talk now,

Pickett?"

"Yes, I would. I was not there by choice. First, I was drugged. And then, when I awoke, I was in the middle of this mess. I had barely gotten oriented when I was nabbed by the DSF MPs."

"What were the illegal activities?" I asked again.

"Sir," Tobias spoke up. "Spaceman Pickett was entangled with a drug cartel. I have very little information about this cartel, but apparently they were smuggling drugs into UME territory from Dalton Spaceways. You would need to go to DSI for more information. In relation to Spaceman Pickett's claim of being drugged, he was tested for drugs by the MPs and found positive for a concoction known as Red Ocean, a very nasty drug. The drug severely damages reflexes and eventually destroys the brain, but supposedly gives a wonderful high."

"Well, I don't want this man on my ship, especially not in the engineering spaces. Please hand him back over to the DSF MPs and tell them to work his case through the SF. I don't have time to deal with it."

"Captain, I'm innocent," Pickett said, as Tobias started to force him out the door.

"Maybe," I said. "But I don't think so, and I don't want someone impaired by Red Ocean working in my engineering spaces. Dismissed."

After they left, Commander Shey Hunter walked through the hatch, with Chief Petty Officer Westell and Spaceman First Class Rio.

"I see from Commander Dale's notes," I said, referring to the notes that Dale had left from the XO screening, "that Commander Hunter is charging Spaceman First Class Rio with criminal neglect. Why?"

"I was running a scheduled drill. During the drill, my spacecraft started leaking reaction mass. Rio is the man in charge of my spacecraft, I believe that he had something to do with the leak."

"Commander," I asked, "do you have any proof?"

"No, sir," Shey responded. "However, he is the only one allowed to touch my spacecraft. I am requesting a JAG investigation."

"Commander, have you had any problems with Spaceman First Class Rio before?"

"Yes, sir," she said without hesitation. "I have never believed he kept my fighter in proper order."

"Chief Westell," I said, turning to Rio's chief petty officer. "What is your impression of Spaceman Rio?"

"Sir," he said, glancing sharply at Shey. "I have tried on multiple occasions over the past couple of months to promote Rio to petty officer third class. Commander Hunter has denied my request every time. I believe that Rio is among the best spacecraft mechanics that I have on my team. Commodore Drove was the one who okayed his promotion to first class. Rio was in charge of the Commodore's Tomcat."

"The rest of you please step outside. I need to confer with Commander Hunter alone."

Once they left, I turned on Shey.

"Shey, you have been nothing but a headache since you came aboard. Jack says you're the best aviator in the Force. Your ribbons prove that, but you're an idiot when it comes to everything else. Rio is a good man. Commodore Drove only allowed the best to touch his Tomcat, so if Rio was his mechanic, then he is the best. I will put Petty Officer Westell personally in charge of your spacecraft. Rio will be promoted to petty officer third class, and he will be placed in charge of another spacecraft. Westell is among the best mechanics we have. He *will* take care of your ship properly. I do not want to hear any more complaints from you. Is that understood *Commander*?"

"Sir, yes, sir."

Shey turned to exit the room.

"Shey." She turned around to look at me. "I do have the power to *permanently* ground you. Don't make me do it. This op we're about to go on is your last chance. Screw this up, and you will *never* be in the cockpit of a fighter *ever* again. Is that understood?"

"Sir, yes, sir!" she spat, her voice dripping with contempt.

Once she was gone, I called the others back in and informed them of the change and congratulated Rio on his promotion to third class.

***

The day finally arrived for testing the cloaking device, but it didn't end well.

"Are you ready?" I commed to engineering from the bridge.

"Yes, sir," Duval said.

"Turn on the cloaking device, Jade."

"Turning on the cloaking device."

"It's on," a watchstander called out.

"Dalton Spaceways is reporting that we are no longer on their scanners," Emily said from her station at comms.

"Good. It looks like you did it, Alex."

"Yes…" he said but was interrupted by an explosion I heard in the background. He swore. "I need a damage control team and a medic here fast!"

"Dalton Spaceways is reporting that we are back on their scanners."

"The controls up here say that the device is still on," Jade said.

I swore in Canid. "Turn it off. I'm heading down to engineering. Jade, you have the deck."

I left the bridge before Jade could confirm her control of the deck. I arrived in engineering to find the place a mess. There had been a huge explosion, and it looked like almost half of the engineering shift was down. The damage control team had quickly put out the fire, but this was not what we needed right before a major op.

I left engineering and rushed to my stateroom. Within three minutes of the failed test, I had Richard on a secure channel.

"Richard," I began. "When you left the *Starwarden*, you told me to tell you if Duval was keeping your engineering spaces in order."

"Yeah," Richard said.

"Well, he needs help." I then proceeded to explain the news.

"Okay," he said. "I'll be down there with a crew in half an hour. I'll get the engineering spaces in shape before the mission. Don't worry."

But I did worry. My only squad mate who had survived London Proper was relying on me. If the *Starwarden* wasn't ready, he was going to blow up the *Marx*, and take himself with it. I couldn't allow that to happen. I couldn't allow my last squad mate to die.

Chapter 7
George McCloud

One week before the big day, Major George McCloud was scheduled to escort a general around the Mars construction port. McCloud was head of dock security at the ship construction facility and met the general as he exited the small UME shuttle.

"General," he said, saluting.

"Major." The general returned the salute. "Is the device on?"

"Yes, sir," McCloud said. They were referring to the noise filter McCloud wore to allow them to communicate in private.

"Good," the general said. He was also a member of the Caledonian Cabal. "We lost track of the Long-Range Tornado once it left the solar system. We've had no contact since then. However, less than twenty minutes after we had estimated Lieutenant Kendrick would arrive, the Solar Fleet's flagship FSAS *Starwarden* jumped back to Sol System, as close to Dalton Spaceways as physically possible. In fact, so close that it took ten tugs to slow her down before she reached Dalton Spaceways. We detected a lot of activity around the *Starwarden*. G2 command believes that she will not come, though."

"Why?" McCloud asked. His hopes had been raised when he heard the *Starwarden* had jumped back to earth, but they were smashed by the general's last words.

"It appears that they're doing major work on the *Starwarden*, and G2 Command believes she's not currently spaceworthy. They've also had past experience with Jack Dalton. They do not believe that Mr. Dalton would okay the mission."

"But isn't the Sky Marshal in command?"

"Our sources are mixed on that," the general said. "We've intercepted multiple communications that mention the 'Big Three.' Most within the UME believe that refers to Sky Marshal Kitt, Jack

Dalton, and the Chairman of the Presidential Council."

"What does G2 think?" McCloud asked.

"We believe that, in fact, it refers to Sky Marshal Kitt, Jack Dalton, and an alien."

"An alien?"

"Yes, we have reason to believe that the Solar Fleet has allied themselves with aliens. We have no proof, but we have heard some odd names. The UME believes they're code words while we believe them to be aliens. 'Passerine,' 'Canid,' 'Zarc,' and 'Ancient Enemy' or 'Ancient Ones.'"

"Anyway," McCloud said, "this is all interesting, but is the Solar Fleet going to help me?"

"I believe they will, but command does not."

McCloud pondered the news while he escorted the general around the base. They made small talk once McCloud turned off the filter, and they didn't discuss the cabal again while the general was on Mars. It wasn't until the general left—one day before the planned hijacking—that McCloud would be able to pass on the news to the fifty other cabal members on the base.

***

"Do you think the Solar Fleet is going to be up there?" a member of G2 asked McCloud in their final meeting before the planned hijacking.

"The general, and I have faith that Almek will come," McCloud said. "However, that doesn't mean I won't prepare for the worst."

"Of course not," Sergeant Delgetty said.

"Are you all prepared to die for the cabal?" McCloud asked his squad of cabal members.

They all looked around at each other, then they all looked up at McCloud. Each of them nodded solemnly. They were prepared to face whatever would come. They were united against the UME and ready to strike a blow against the UME even if they risked losing their lives.

"Good," McCloud said.

He sat down and began to outline the final plan to his men. Once the meeting was over, he would have to meet up with one of the two members of the cabal serving on the *Marx*. He had to make sure they understood everything precisely. He couldn't afford to have anyone mess up even a small detail. McCloud was ready to avenge Kathy and all the others whom the UME had ruthlessly slaughtered in the London Proper Detention Facility. At least he would no longer be part of the UME. He would rather die than serve these murdering bastards another day. Tomorrow, he would fight for his freedom again like he had done at Kathy's side in London Proper.

He could only hope that Almek would return, as he had promised, to help his last squad mate still in the UME. His fate was back in the hands of his old squad leader, just like the old days.

***

Major George McCloud got up the next morning, anxious and ready to go. All the planning and all the hard work were about to culminate in an amazing escape or a blinding explosion. He dressed faster than normal, gulped down two mugs of coffee to get the caffeine going through his system, and went to wake up the rest of his patrol.

McCloud was in position. His ten-man squad was doing its normal dockside patrol in the early hours of the morning, at 0500 to be precise. His earbud beeped, and he touched it to accept the call.

"Major McCloud, we're in position," Lieutenant Kelso said. That meant Kelso was out of sight of the *Marx* but within fifty meters of her.

McCloud couldn't respond since there were two people in his patrol who weren't part of the cabal. Kelso just had to trust that

McCloud had received the message. McCloud's squad continued walking the dockside patrol. McCloud scanned the roads and the docks, and no one else was around. The plan seemed to be working perfectly so far.

It was 0530 when his squad reached the *Marx*. He held up his hand in a fist, and his patrol stopped behind him. The members of the cabal understood that the mission was now officially a go. There would be no turning back in a matter of seconds.

"What is it, sir?" McCloud's lieutenant, who wasn't a member of the cabal, asked.

"One second, Lieutenant," McCloud said. He pushed his earbud again.

"This is G2 command, do you copy Major McCloud?"

"This is Major McCloud, I copy," McCloud replied.

"Are your men in position, Major?"

"Yes, sir."

"We still do not know for certain if you're going to have any help from the Solar Fleet. Even if you can only destroy the *Marx*, it will still be a victory for the cabal. G2 is grateful for your dedication."

It was clear to McCloud that command still assumed this would be a suicide mission. McCloud trusted that Almek would help if he were in a position to do so. The question was whether or not Almek would be in a favorable position. As command had told them last week, they weren't even certain if Lieutenant Kendrick had reached Almek.

"We'll check it out," McCloud said. He drew his sidearm, spun around, and put two rounds into his UME lieutenant. Sergeant Delgetty took down the other UME scum that was on McCloud's team. "Okay," McCloud said, turning to the members of the cabal. "Let's do this for our loved ones and for the freedom of Scotland and Ireland!"

The other cabal members ran over to McCloud's squad from

different hiding spots and rushed up the quarterdeck after McCloud killed the ensign standing in-port watch on the *Marx*. They quickly boarded the ship. McCloud split his squad into teams of two, and they headed through the ship killing everyone who wasn't a member of the cabal. McCloud and Delgetty made a beeline for the bridge. Delgetty made quick work of the captain as he came out of his stateroom trying to figure out what was going on. One shot to the head.

They arrived on the bridge and saw that the executive officer and the navigator were in position.

"Do we have all of the command codes?" McCloud asked the exec.

"Yes, sir."

"Engineering?" McCloud called out over the ship intercom.

"We have engineering. We're ready to go," Lieutenant Kelso replied.

"Let's take her up, nav," McCloud said.

"Will do."

The ship slowly rose from its land-based dock, rising toward the red sky over Mars.

"All engineering systems are working fine," Kelso reported a couple of minutes later.

"We're exiting atmo now," the navigator said.

"Scans are only picking up UME ships. I have no signs of Solar Fleet ships. It looks like we're in suicide mode," the exec said.

"Sir," Delgetty said. "UME monarchs are ordering us to return to our dock or be fired upon."

"Kelso," McCloud ordered. "Prepare the reactor core to overload. We're going to try and make a run for it, but if we have to go down, we'll take the ship with us. Delgetty, don't respond to the channel. Nav, what's your name?"

The man turned to face him. "I'm Lieutenant Daniel Lee."

"Lee," McCloud said. "Push this ship for all it's worth. We'll win our Creag Choinnich race or spit blood trying!"

"Sir," the exec said. "They're charging lasers."

"They've given us ten seconds notice," Delgetty said.

"For the Caledonian Cabal!" McCloud shouted. "Delgetty, get to the weapons. Let's fire first."

The *Marx* was able to take down two light cruisers before the UME started firing on them. They'd taken advantage of surprise and would leave a scar on the UME before going nova.

"Lieutenant Lee," McCloud said. "How much further?"

"I need five more minutes," he said.

"Our shields can't take this much longer," Delgetty said from the weapons console.

"Engineering, prepare to overload the core on my mark," McCloud said. "Let's go down with style!"

He had trusted Almek for the last time, and he just hoped that Almek had a good reason for not showing. For Caledonia and Kathy, McCloud thought.

Chapter 8
Escape to Colony One

"Commander Duval," I said, as calmly as I could. "We have to leave in an hour and forty-five minutes."

"Sir," Duval said. "We're doing our best."

"When will you be finished?"

"We're looking at an hour and a half, sir."

"Get it done, then."

I decided I'd better go down to engineering to check on the problem. Richard, Duval, and a team of snipes had locked themselves into the Kelven space for the past two weeks, trying to make the *Starwarden* battle worthy.

The *Starwarden* had three engineering spaces. The main engineering space housed the matter-antimatter reactor core, along with the life support systems. The next largest engineering space held the Kelven Drive, the cloaking device, and the navigation and guidance systems. And the smallest engineering space housed the human-designed matter-conversion drive. The matter-conversion drive was the back-up power system and was capable of powering all the life support systems. When the cloaking device exploded, it had damaged the K-drive and most of the electronics housed in that space.

I pushed the hatch buzzer and tried to open the hatch. It was locked. I used my implant to override the lock, opened the hatch and walked into an engineering nightmare. The K-drive was normally housed in a large metal framework. At the moment, that box was open and parts were strewn across the floor. I heard loud banging coming from inside the box.

"Winters, Duval," I called out to my top engineers.

I heard Richard swearing from inside the K-drive. I walked over to the open side of the framework and saw Richard inside. I quickly looked for Duval and found him and the other snipes working on the cloaking device, which the massive K-drive had blocked from my view. I watched Richard work on the drive. He delicately moved wires from place to place, tearing out some and cross-wiring others. I was glad that I knew him well. There were only a handful of people who understood the inner workings of the K-drive. With his combination of R&D theory plus practical know-how from having bossed Starwarden's engineering spaces, Richard just couldn't be topped. The Fleet and DSI produced many Kelven drives, but there were few engineers who could match Richard's understanding of the drive. And since the *Starwarden* had the most advanced K-drive ever built, its drive couldn't just be replaced with a spare from the parts closet. It had to be repaired, or we would manage no better than a sub-light crawl.

"OK, test it!" Richard shouted, holding a wire in place with one hand while shorting a metal pad to a cluster of wires with his boot.

"Running test," a snipe shouted.

Sparks jumped off the metal pad, while Richard yelled, "Keep her going!" A large puff of smoke obscured Richard for a second. "Cut it off!" Richard ordered and started swearing as another puff of smoke emerged. Richard kept swearing until the smoke cleared, and then he saw me.

"Is it going to be ready?" I asked.

"Almek," Richard said. "With all due respect, get the hell out of my engineering space. I'll tell you when I have something to tell you. You have no useful experience. So get out my deck and stay out of the way."

***

"Is it done yet?" I asked from my post back on the bridge. It was five minutes past our scheduled departure time, and I could honor Richard's demand for peace no longer.

"Sir, we …"

"Duval, I don't want excuses. The people of the cabal will act in one hour. And we have ten minutes left to have a chance of reaching support range even at the top K we can do while cloaked."

"Sir, we're doing the last tweaks to the system right now."

"Finish it up," I ordered. "I'm preparing to jump."

"Sir," Duval said. "We have a constructor still making adjustments to our hull."

"He better be off in ten minutes, because that's when we're jumping." I turned to face Jade, who had the watch. "Jade, prepare for undock and jump."

"Will do," Jade said, acknowledging my order. "BM, retract the quarterdeck. Release mooring lines. Let's get this ship moving."

It was good to know that at least some people were eager to go.

"Snipes," I muttered under my breath.

"Can't live with 'em, can't live without 'em," Jade said with a tense grin. "The rest of the ship is ready, sir."

"Sonnel," I said, opening a channel to the *Zochtil*, which was standing by with a small flotilla of cruisers and grapeshot frigates, including the one captained by Lauren.

"The *Zochtil* is ready, Almek. We can have a wormhole open in thirty seconds."

"Good," I said, closing the channel and calling up engineering again. "Duval, do we at least have the K-drive back up?"

"One second … yes. The K-drive is operational," he said, drawing out the last word.

"Can you make the remaining repairs while flying FTL?"

"No, sir," Duval said. "I must have the constructor."

"Duval, we're past deadline. I don't care if we have to throw a big blanket over the ship to cloak it. We need to go now!"

"We're working on it, *sir*."

"Duval, get off the channel. I want Richard."

"Richard here, Captain."

"Richard, lives are riding on this."

"Sir," Richard said, sounding calmer than I felt. "I am moving as fast as possible. I just got a red light on one of the inertial dampers. Give me time."

"Richard, time is the one thing we don't have."

***

"Engineering," I practically hissed. "We should have left thirty minutes ago. Richard, you want us to lose that monarch? We need to move."

"Almost ready. Give us fifteen minutes, and we can go."

I swore in as many languages as I knew. "Jade, plot an updated course. We'll travel at top K. I want to be on top of the UME."

Jade nodded. "I already did that, sir. I plotted the two courses yesterday, one assuming we got out on time, the other assuming we left at the last possible minute."

I laughed. "That's why I like you a lot better than those snipes. Good job, Jade. I will make record of this in your file."

Ten minutes later, Richard finally announced, "We're good to go, sir. The constructor is out of range."

"Jade…" I began, but before I could even finish saying her name, she was giving orders to leave. Jade had the *Starwarden* going at K speeds in a mater of seconds.

The boatswain's mate sounded General Quarters, and I used my implant to do a quick check. I wanted to make sure everyone was at their battle stations. All the weapons were manned, and the fighters were standing by, ready to launch.

"Let's do this," I said.

***

We arrived seven and a half minutes after the time the cabal had planned for starting the op. It took a couple seconds for the sensors to recalibrate, and when they did, we saw the *Marx* running the gauntlet with three Monarchs crawling all over her.

"Open fire!" I ordered. "Launch all fighters!" *Shey, this is you only chance. Show me that you're worth those medals on your chest.*

The Monarchs weren't expecting the Solar Fleet to show up, so their ships hadn't bothered to charge up their phasing drive. The *Starwarden* had come in with her antimatter torpedo tubes firing on full automatic. Within fifteen seconds, the three Monarchs were down, and Shey had the fighters and bombers tearing into the smaller craft.

***

"Sir," Kelso called out from engineering. "I think I've got the phasing drive charged up. You can use it from the bridge."

"Good," McCloud said. "Maybe that will buy us time to escape, but stand ready to slam the core into overload."

"Sir!" Delgetty shouted. "We have a Solar Fleet ship on our scanners."

McCloud leaned forward in his chair and said a quick prayer of thanks. They might survive after all.

"Just one ship?" the executive officer asked.

"Yes," Delgetty said. "Sir! They just took out all three Monarchs."

"They what … how?" McCloud tried to ask, sitting up straight. "Three Monarchs in a mater of seconds?"

"Yes, sir."

***

"The fire on the *Marx* has reduced significantly," Jade informed me. "We're picking up signs of more ships launching from the surface. We also have two more Monarchs coming around from either side of the planet. Sensors are detecting their phasing drives are online."

"It looks like we've worn out our welcome," I said. "Open a comm channel with the *Marx*."

"I've got it, sir," Emily said. "You're on."

"This is Captain Almek Manning. I've been informed that you and your people would like to request asylum."

"Almek!" McCloud shouted. "It's good to see you, but you did cut it awfully close."

"We're not out of the heat yet," I said. "Don't worry about the other UME vessels. My crew and I will deal with them. Just get yourself outta here. My comm officer is sending you the coordinates for our rendezvous point. We'll join you as soon as possible."

"My comm officer has received the coordinates," McCloud said. "Are you sure you can't use our help?"

"McCloud, we are here to make sure your ship escapes intact. We'll worry about the enemy. You get out of here."

"Will do, Squad Lead."

"The *Marx* needs another two minutes before she can jump to FTL," Jade said.

"Let's keep up the fight for that long then," I acknowledged.

I turned my gaze to the holodisplay of the battlefield. I had to admit Shey had worked wonders in combat. I'd thought that Kai was a good aviator and CAG, but Shey was, indeed, a master in the field. I watched her customized spacecraft weave in between enemy ships, dodging missiles and debris as if by instinct. It truly seemed she was wearing her spacecraft rather than piloting it. The two Monarchs that had come from the opposite side of Mars were now within firing range, and they opened fire.

"I want a spread of antimatter torpedoes launched at the closest Monarch. Get a lock on it with the phasic shield," I ordered.

"I have a lock," a watchstander shouted.

Two of the torpedoes hit, then the lock died, and the ship phased out again.

"I need you to lock longer than that!" I shouted.

"I've got a lock again."

Fortunately, there were still torpedoes on course. Two more hit, and the Monarch was destroyed. The phasic shield generator was being aimed again when the *Starwarden* took a hit.

"I've lost the phasic shield generator!" the same watchstander shouted.

"Engineering, I just lost the phasic shield generator," I repeated.

"It must have been shot off," Duval said. "I've lost all readings from it down here."

I swore. "Has the *Marx* jumped yet?" I asked.

"They're charging up their drive," Jade said. "The UME is using a much older version of the K drive. They should be able to jump in about thirty seconds."

"Okay," I said. "Charge up our drive. Let's get out of here. All fighters RTB!"

"The *Marx* is gone!" a watchstander shouted.

"Then let's disappear too."

I heard Jade run down the checklist of systems before we jumped. We were retreating at just under light speed, when I heard Jade give the order to jump followed by the familiar whir from the drives and then a massive crunching noise.

"What just happened?" I asked, as I put my head into my hands.

"Something just happened to the drive, sir," Richard reported. "I'm not sure exactly what, but we're lucky to be alive."

"We won't be much longer if we can't bypass light speed."

"Sir," Jade said. "We now have five Monarchs on our tail. Four more came up from the surface to join the fun."

"Richard, can you fix it in sixty seconds?"

"No, sir."

"*Zochtil!*" I called out.

"This is the *Zochtil*."

"I need a wormhole right now."

"Roger. We'll jump to you," the Canid confirmed, "and then jump both of us back."

"Great! Make it fast."

We kept running for another minute, before one of the Monarchs decided to jump to K-speed and get ahead of us. They ended up right ahead of us, as the wormhole opened on top of them, and their ship was torn to pieces. Even *Starwarden* barely avoided the wormhole when the *Zochtil* appeared in front of us. The inbound wormhole closed and another started opening.

One-and-a-half minutes later, we were back in L5 orbit over earth. From there, the *Zochtil* opened another wormhole to the rendezvous, and our two ships went through to meet up with the *Marx*.

Chapter 9
Another Run-in with Daniel Lee

"We'll be exiting the wormhole in thirty seconds," a watchstander informed me.

"Okay," I acknowledged. "Bronski, come in."

"Bronski, here."

"You guys ready to board a Monarch?"

"Hooyah!" Bronski shouted. "We've been waiting for way too long."

"Now's your chance. Be ready for anything. I want to trust this cabal, but I'm not going to risk Colony One. We have to make sure there isn't any foul play here."

"Exiting the wormhole now."

"Sir," Jade said, looking up sharply at me. "The *Marx* isn't here."

I swore. "Then again, maybe not, Bronski. They aren't here."

"Jade, you're the nav. Look into the jump records. I thought we'd confirmed their jump bearings."

"I'm already on it, sir."

"The records confirm this was their destination," Jade said, after rerunning the calculations. "They should be here unless they managed to jump again.

"Bridge, this is CIC."

"We copy, CIC," I said.

"Sir," Kris Taggart began. "This definitely *was* their destination."

"But they aren't here any more," Jade said.

"You mean they aren't here yet. Remember, the reconstructions we did after the Battle for the Orbitals projected their max speed as K-2. If they haven't improved since then, they should arrive in five to ten minutes."

"Wow, that is slow," I said. "I'm glad we've got snipes like Richard improving our drive."

"Amen," Jade said. "K-2 is impossibly slow."

We waited impatiently for the *Marx* to show up.

"We have an incoming channel," Emily said.

"How did you get here so fast?" McCloud asked.

"Better tech," I said. "We've been here eight minutes."

"Your ship looks pretty beat up."

"It is," I confirmed. "We just finished up repairs on her from the last battle. She's probably due for another three or four months of dry dock again."

"Sorry for causing so much trouble."

"Don't worry," I said. "Thanks for giving me an excuse to rescue a squad mate."

"I noticed you picked an uninhabited system," McCloud said. "I assume you'll want to run an inspection to make sure we are who we say we are."

"I'd say the Battle over Mars established *your* creds," I replied. "But I still have to make sure the ship isn't rigged."

"How do you want to do this?" McCloud asked. "Do you want me to come within airlock range?"

"I've got a spec ops boarding team headed your way. There are aliens on the team, so don't freak out."

"So, the general was right," McCloud said, almost to himself.

"Excuse me?"

"Oh," McCloud said. "One of the cabal members came by last week. He said G2 believed that the Solar Fleet had allied with aliens."

"That is true," I said. "The aliens who will be boarding your ship are called Passerines. They look like angels, but don't fire on them, or they *will* kill you. These guys have captured multiple Draconian ships, so they're the best."

"You've captured Draconian ships?" McCloud asked.

"We can discuss everything in greater detail once we jump out of here. Just be patient."

"Aye, aye, sir."

"Bronski," I said once I had closed the channel with McCloud. "You have a go. I want your camera continually transmitting back to me."

"Will do."

I flipped from the holodisplay of the system to a holo of the world as seen through Zach Bronski's implant. I watched his specialized docking ship land on an airlock and force it open. Then, Bronski's team of STARs swarmed into the passageway. Scourge took point, while Ed stayed back with the ship. Bronski kept looking from side to side. Though I believed that everything would be fine, Bronski was obviously looking for trouble.

Bronski's team ran into one of the Wingman teams on the way. The Wingman team was tasked with scanning engineering, while Bronski's objective was the bridge. His team reached the bridge without any trouble. Thomas slapped a control console to the hatch leading to the bridge. In a matter of seconds, Thomas had overridden the controls, and the door slid open.

"EVERYBODY ON THE FLOOR!" Scourge shouted. "Anyone who moves without being told will be killed."

Bronski walked in behind Scourge. All of the men had complied with Scourge's orders. Not that anyone in their right mind would disobey Scourge. Although Scourge wasn't anywhere near the height of a Passerine, he still towered over most humans. Even without body armor, Scourge was bulky and well muscled. Throw full STAR body armor on, give him a helmet, and a nasty looking SCAR rifle, and he was downright terrifying. And if all that wasn't enough, you hear him yelling at you in his gravelly voice, and you *are* going to obey whatever that man tells you to do.

Bronski let his own SCAR drop to his side, as he inspected the bridge. Thomas went straight to the captain's chair and started running diagnostics.

It looks clear from here, Thomas linked after a couple minutes.

Okay, Bronski linked. "Gramnol," Bronski said, holding his hand to his earbud.

"Gramnol here," the Passerine leader of the first Wingman squad replied.

"What does engineering look like?"

"Looks okay," he said. "I've got a Lieutenant Kelso here who is helping my team cool down the reactor. They had it set to overload in case they couldn't make it out of Mars orbit. Besides that, we're clear down here."

"Yognol," Bronski said, calling the leader of the second Wingman squad. "Any bombs?"

"Still working on that, sir," the Passerine replied. "It's a big ship. So far, everything looks good, though."

"I copy." Bronski turned to the prisoners, who were still lying face down on the floor, arms spread-eagled. "Okay, which one of you is George McCloud?"

"Can we get up?" McCloud asked. "Or do you just want to interview us on our stomachs?"

"*You* can get up, McCloud," Bronski said. "But don't make any sudden moves."

"Wouldn't dream of it," McCloud said, as he slowly raised himself to a kneeling position on the deck.

"Introduce me to your bridge crew," Bronski ordered. "They are *not* to get up. I just want names that we can cross reference with our database."

"Okay," McCloud said. "I've got Sergeant Scott Delgetty. He's my right hand man. Then over there is…"

McCloud went on to introduce the other members of his team who were on the bridge. There were fourteen of them on the bridge, and so far none of them had triggered any major bells when their names were checked. All of them were UME soldiers, but we had already known that. Then McCloud came to the last cabal member on the bridge.

"That man over there is the second of my naval cabal contacts. I can't vouch for him personally, but he is a certified cabal member."

"I don't want his life story," Bronski said. "Just give me his name."

"His last name is Lee," McCloud said, "and I think his first name is Daniel."

My heart skipped a beat. It couldn't be? It had to be a coincidence. How could Daniel Lee have wound up in the Caledonian Cabal? However, Scourge didn't treat it as a coincidence.

"Get up now, Lee!" Scourge roared at the man.

He slowly obeyed Scourge's order, and as soon as he was standing up, Scourge charged him, grabbed him by the neck, and flung him into the hallway. Before Lee could get up, Scourge was lifting him up and holding him to the bulkhead of the hallway.

"You make a move I think is even the slightest bit funny, and I'll shoot you full of holes," Scourge said, jamming the muzzle of his SCAR into the man's chest.

If it had been any other hostage, both Bronski and I would have ordered Scourge to put the man down, but it wasn't just any hostage. It was Daniel Lee. Lee had been my archenemy from Boot Camp to the Academy. At Boot Camp, he seemed to naturally hate me, and I got into a brawl with him that almost cost me my career before it even got started. Then he mutinied on my ship during the final sim. The Sky Marshal asked for my advice on what to do with him. I myself had come dangerously close to mutiny in one of the sims, so I suggested that the Sky Marshal let it slide. And I had regretted that decision ever since.

At the Academy, things only escalated. We had many verbal duels, and then my SAP was sabotaged during my qualifying run. Sonnel found evidence that Lee was responsible, but it couldn't be proven. And then, during our last couple months at the Academy, Lee rigged one of the tubes to the outer rings to blow while I was on it. My friends and I had barely escaped with our lives, but Lee had neatly escaped in a viper. We weren't sure where he had run off to, but now we knew.

"You guys never saw this coming, did you?" Lee asked. "Thought I was gone for good? Well, you thought wrong, didn't you?"

"Bronski," I said into his earbud, "I want you to triple check everything. If Daniel Lee is on this ship, then something is seriously wrong here. I'm sending over a bomb squad now."

*I agree with yo*u, Bronski said over his implant so that Lee wouldn't hear him. *Everything in this ship will be double-checked millimeter by millimeter.* Bronski walked out into the hallway to face Lee.

"I've wanted to see you for a long time," Bronski said. "You almost got me killed with that stunt you pulled at the Academy. You're going to get hit hard once we take you back to the Solar Fleet. You'll die after they put you through the formality of a court martial."

"No. *You* will," Daniel said. "I was hoping that Almek himself would board the ship. He always pretended to be a hands-on leader, but maybe command has changed him." Daniel shrugged. "I guess the Fleet's best spec ops team will have to do."

"Kill him now!" I shouted.

Scourge and Bronski opened fire on Daniel, but it was too late. Daniel had bit down hard, and Bronski's implant detected traces of a poisonous gas. I saw his armor instantly seal up and start using it's own oxygen supply, but it was too late.

Thomas, I said, as I linked with him. *Get that door closed and shut down the ventilation systems now!*

"On it," he said. He'd jumped towards one of the consoles and was now pounding away at it.

I saw the emergency hatches on either side of Bronski, Scourge, and Lee slide shut.

"I want a hazmat team over there now," I said. The readings I was getting from Bronski's implant didn't look good. Bronski and Scourge were the only ones directly exposed to the gas. Thomas had everyone evacuate the bridge, while Thomas tried to vent the atmo in the hallway to space and pump in clean air.

The hazmat team arrived ten minutes later. SAPs were just so insufferably slow! They did all they could, but the gas wouldn't move. We weren't sure of its properties, but it seemed to keep reforming as soon as we filled the hallway with breathable air. Thomas was getting very frustrated, but I wasn't paying attention to him. I was worried about the rest of the STAR team.

Though the gas seemed to be able to reform in the hallway, it hadn't reached the team on the bridge, since Thomas had made it to the ventilation controls in time. However, my hazmat officer wasn't sure what to do with the team in the hallway.

"It isn't a poison the Fleet, DSI, Canids, or Passerines have dealt with before," she told me via a comm channel. "Without getting samples of the poison, which I don't recommend, I can't help them. The only thing on their side is the nanos that come with the implants. The nanos may be able to fight it, but I can't help them."

"I understand," I said. "Try to help Thomas vent the gas."

"Understood, sir."

"Emily," I said, turning to my comm officer. "I need a secure link with Colony One Space Command."

"You're on, Captain."

"Admiral Smith," I said. "This is Captain Almek Manning."

"Captain Manning," Smith said. "Were there any complications, or are you preparing to jump back"

"There were complications. The ship is in one piece, but right now I can't place a crew aboard. I'll need to have tugs bring us in."

"Almek, my tugs can't go at K-speeds."

"Oh, sorry," I said. "My K-drive got fried. I have the *Zochtil* with me now to help with the jump."

"Okay," Smith said, as he took in the scene. "I'll have the *Tycoon* headed you're way with about thirty tugs."

"Sounds good. Thanks for the help."

***

By the time the *Tycoon* arrived an hour later, we still hadn't made any progress on the gas. The tugs moved smoothly into position around the *Marx* and did a test burn that sent the ship spinning. They adjusted their position and tested again. This time she flew straight.

"We're ready," the captain in charge of the tug flotilla confirmed.

"*Zochtil*," I said. "Warm up the wormhole. We're headed to Colony One."

"Okay. Let's get out of here."

***

One day later, a squad of four people entered the hallway outside the bridge while it was in vacuum. They walked over to the body of Daniel Lee and put him onto a makeshift operating table. Then they slowly began an autopsy.

It was grizzly watching the doctors gut him in vacuum. After half an hour, I heard an exclamation from one of the docs.

"What's up?" I asked immediately.

"We found out why the gas keeps coming back," the doctor said.

"Why?"

He pulled something out of Lee's ear.

"I'm no engineer," the doctor said. "But it looks to me like this thing was designed to create the gas."

"Have you found anything else?" I asked.

"Yes," another doctor said. He reached into the lungs, grabbed something, and brought it out. "This may be a filter of some kind. I don't think Lee would've died from breathing the gas."

"I've got a question for you guys," I said. "What kind of tech is this?"

"Nanos," Ardent said from behind me. "That is the only explanation. If the UME has access to Ancient technology, then they most likely have access to advanced nanotechnology too."

"Thank you, Ardent," I said, then addressed the doctors again. "One of my executive officers believes it could be nanos. I want both of those things stored in vacuum chambers, and I want the body stored in a body bag."

"Will do."

Though I had never liked Daniel Lee, I still didn't like what I had to do next. I had the body bag jettisoned from a SAP then one of my Passerine fighters zapped it with an antimatter beam. The body and anything else it may have carried was gone forever. Lee would never bother me or my squad again. I only regretted not being able to unravel the majority of Lee's story.

***

Not long after that, I was in a meeting with the Big Three above Colony One.

"Well," the Sky Marshal said, "the mission appears to have been a success."

"Yes," Richard said. "I've already started running tests on the phasing drive. It's an amazing piece of technology."

"However," Jack Dalton said. "The *Starwarden* took heavy damage."

"Yes," I agreed. "With Richard overseeing things while also doing research, I think the *Starwarden* is going to need at least six months to repair."

"I'd agree with that," Richard said. "The Kelven drive is completely fried. I'll have to start from scratch on the new one. Six months to refit the *Starwarden* may be a conservative estimate."

"We almost lost one of my best STAR teams, too," the Sky Marshal said. "How are they doing now?"

"Bronski and Scourge will recover," I said. "The doctors tell me that the nanos are working overtime to repair their systems. It will take months, though. The poison that Lee used was extremely toxic and, without nanotechnology, they would have been dead. However, they will make a full recovery."

"Good," the Sky Marshal said. "That was way too close for comfort. We can't afford to lose Bronski or Scourge."

"What about the *Marx*?" Numair asked. "What do you intend to do with her?"

"I'm not sure," the Sky Marshal replied.

"I'd like to re-commission her as an FSA ship," Jack said.

"Sir," I asked, "what do you plan to do with the cabal members?"

"They'd be useless to the cabal now," the Sky Marshal said. "We'll have to absorb them into the Fleet, provided they pass the psych exam."

"May I make a request?" I asked.

The Sky Marshal raised an eyebrow at me. "You're asking to make a request? Were you exposed to the gas?"

"Fire away," Jack said, smiling at me.

"I think that we should transfer George McCloud to the Fleet and allow him to command the *Marx*."

"What!" the Sky Marshal exclaimed. "You want us to entrust our prize ship to a cabal member?"

"He's trustworthy," Jack said, surprising me by speaking up for McCloud. "If it weren't for him, we wouldn't have the *Marx* right now. We can trust him with the ship after he passes the psych exams."

"You agree with Manning?" the Sky Marshal asked.

"I do, too," Numair said. "We need to allow this G2 or Caledonian Cabal to officially join our alliance. To do that, they need to have a ship. Let McCloud hold his rank of Major, but allow him to skipper the ship. There's Passerine precedent for marines commanding ships. We have a couple major-skippers and even more colonel-skippers."

"Sonnel?" the Sky Marshal asked, still hoping someone would back him.

"I agree with the rest of them. We need this cabal's help to defeat the UME, so we can move on to the Draconian threat."

"We're supposed to trust McCloud with this ship?" the Sky Marshal asked with incredulity, still not willing to admit that he was outnumbered.

"It's decided," Jack said. "I'll make the needed arrangements. However, we'll have to rechristen her, and we'll need to upgrade her. Richard?"

"I've got my hands full with the *Starwarden* and the new phasing drive, but I do have a couple friends I can recommend. I will, of course, help with the Kelven drive when you're ready to upgrade that. I believe that we need to stay here in orbit around Colony One. They have more than competent facilities here, and that will keep the enemy guessing."

"I agree," Jack said, "but have you heard that Colony One now has a name?"

"What?" I asked. "I thought Colony One was its name?"

"The population has exploded. Colony doesn't seem like the right name for it anymore. The locals elected senators, who managed to keep their noses out of taxes and regulations long enough to come up with a name."

"So, what is it?" Richard asked.

"Branson."

"As in Sir Richard Branson?" I asked. "The founder of commercial space flight?"

"Yes," Jack said. "They're also no longer under the control of DSI. I want the free market to flourish. Of course, right now, I'm still the main provider of jobs, but I have no wish to own planets. I'm perfectly content just with Dalton Spaceways."

I laughed. "Yeah, because that's such a small thing to own. Anyway, I think it would be good for crew morale to stay here. It will be easier to grant leave planet-side here than on Earth. Though I don't understand why people would ever want to leave space, most humans seem to be emotionally attached to solid ground."

"Almek," Jack said. "Are you sure you don't want to transfer to the Space Force? You're a man much like myself."

"Does it make a difference anymore?" I asked him. "On the *Starwarden,* at least, Space Forcers and Fleet personnel seem to have bonded well."

"True, but when this war is over..."

"I'll worry about that then."

"Okay," Jack said. "Well, unless Richard has an update on defeating the phasing drive, I think we should adjourn this meeting."

"I have nothing yet," Richard said. "Give me two months, and we can meet again."

"Okay then," Jack said, "I have some matters to arrange. I'll talk to all of you later."

As the attendees left, I snagged the Sky Marshal.

"Sky Marshal," I asked, "can I talk with you?"

"Sure, what's up?"

"What is Nicole Taylor up to?" I asked him. "I can't contact her implant. It's off the network."

"Nicole is currently going through Marine Boot Camp."

"Why?" I asked, surprised.

"Why do you think?" the Sky Marshal responded.

My brain started to fly through the different possibilities before it finally clicked. "Nicole was promoted to commodore after the Battle of the Blockade, right?"

"Yes."

"So you have selected her as the next Sky Marshal?" I asked.

"She's part of my succession plan. Nicole is going through a fast track as a Marine. Only a few are eligible to be Sky Marshal at the moment. I want her to be in the pool if the need arises."

"Thanks for informing me, sir," I said.

"No problem. One day, if you live long enough, you'll be Sky Marshal."

"I hope not, sir. Before I was given command, I dreamed of it, but I no longer have *that* ambition."

"We'll see."

Part 2
Intrasolar Conflict

Chapter 10
Caledonia

"Okay Richard," the Sky Marshal said, "you've had eight months. We need something to work with. The Alliance plans to attack the UME in just four more months."

"And I've finally got answers for you guys," Richard said.

The past eight months had been torture. I'd spent virtually all my time nursing the *Starwarden* back to life. But now she was finally back in fighting shape. Richard had even been able to boost the new Kelven drive. The cloaking field was up and running, and our phasic shield weapon was working most of the time. We even had a phasing drive installed.

The *Starwarden* was ready for combat. We just needed to know that we could actually hit the enemy ships. That was Richard's job, and now we were in a meeting with the Big Three, along with our most courteous Zarc ambassador, who had refused to talk to us for the past five months. In fact, this meeting was called at the last minute, because our Zarc ambassador had suddenly showed up.

"The phasic drive actually works like the seventh dimensional transmitters that the Passerines and Draconians use," Richard began. "They literally push the ship into another dimension. Sound familiar? The question from there is which dimension is the ship getting pushed into? Based on the tests that my team and I have run, we believe that eighty percent of the time the ship is pushed somewhere between the fourth and seventh dimensions. The other twenty percent it goes beyond that. Now does anybody see what that naturally leads to?"

"No, Richard," I told him. "That's why you're the one leading the team. The rest of us don't have doctorates in alien technology."

"I don't have a doctorate in alien tech," Richard said in exasperation. "Anyway, do you guys know how the seventh dimensional transmitter works?"

"No," I repeated. "Just tell us."

"Excuse me, but some of us do," High Admiral Numair said.

I nodded at him, but waved for Richard to continue.

"Well," Richard said, "the transmitter does the same thing the phasic drive does. It transmits a ship through the fourth, fifth, and then sixth dimension before it stops in the seventh. Are you seeing it yet?" Richard paused for dramatic effect. "We strap a seventh dimensional puncher onto a warhead! And we have it punch through right where our target had been. As long as the enemy ship is within the first seven dimensions, it will get hit. Also the tests show that the shields of a ship go down when it is phased out. So, if we hit it while it's phased out, there will be no shields to protect it. If we score a hit, the ship is crippled."

"I like it," the Sky Marshal said.

"I don't," Jack objected. "Do you know how expensive a seventh dimensional puncher is?"

"Yeah," Richard said, shrugging, "but there's no choice...we need them."

"A puncher costs about as much as a Heinlein-class cruiser. We can't strap those onto warheads!"

"You want us to shoot cruisers at the enemy?" the Sky Marshal asked, turning to Richard.

"There's no other way," Richard said. "I've tried everything! Nothing else has a chance of hitting a phased ship. Remember, they're phasing to a different dimension. None of our existing weapons ever leak across dimensional boundaries. That's why we must have the punchers. It's the only way to deliver an inter-dimensional payload."

The Sky Marshal rubbed the back of his neck, then looked back up at Richard. "These aren't even guaranteed to work are they?"

"No, sir. I estimate they'll work about eighty percent of the time."

The Sky Marshal leaned forward, putting his head in his hands and rubbing his temples. We all sat in silence while he thought. Finally, he looked up at me. "We'll put ten on the *Starwarden* and ten on the *Sky*. Richard, these better work. Numair, we need twenty punchers. What can we give you in return?"

"Richard is truly ingenious," Numair said. "No Passerine would have thought of something so ridiculous. We're in this as an Alliance, so we will give you twenty of them, but don't ask for any more than that."

"Deal," the Sky Marshal said. "Jack, can you actually build the warheads?"

"If Richard sends me the specs, I'll build them."

Richard's eyes glazed over as he did something on his implant. "Sent."

"I've got them. Nice design," Jack said a few minutes later. "Beside the fact that it costs a minor fortune. I'll have them completed in a month."

"Good. What about other alien technology?" the Sky Marshal said while facing the cloud of a Zarc ambassador.

"I've answered that before," the Zarc said. "I am not free to give you information about the Phobians. That is not within my authority."

"Couldn't you just accidentally drop a memory orb packed with data?" the Sky Marshal prodded.

"That would count as giving you information," the Zarc said dryly. "We cannot pretend to follow our laws and not do so in reality. That would be wrong and illegal."

"Aliens," the Sky Marshal muttered.

"Well," Jack said, "I believe that we have a christening to attend in just under thirty minutes. We'd better get going."

"True," the Sky Marshal replied, shooting a parting glare at the cloud. "Dismissed."

We'd all gotten up and were headed out the door when our Zarc ambassador spoke.

"I can tell you this," he said from within the misty cloud. "Richard found the only way within your technological ability to defeat the phasing drive. I am impressed."

"Is there a cheaper solution?" Richard asked.

"Yes and no," the Zarc said. "There *is* a cheaper warhead, but it would be more expensive to develop the technological abilities to build it."

"Could you give us just a couple of them?" the Sky Marshal asked.

"I've told you in the past," the Zarc said. "The party that controls our military dislikes us wasting time on you lower-class species. You should appreciate the little information I can give." With that, the Zarc cloud disappeared, leaving only an empty chair.

"Why can't they be just a tad more helpful?" I asked.

It was a rhetorical question and nobody responded.

***

"You ready for this?" I asked Colonel George McCloud. "Joining the Alliance and having your own ship to command? I know you weren't like me. You didn't even want command back in London Proper. And I can't believe I ever wanted it."

"I thought you enjoy commanding the *Starwarden*?"

"Oh, I do," I said. "But command is tough. Are you ready to give up freedom, privacy, and sound sleep?"

"I hope so, Almek. You're right, I'm not like you. After being drafted into the UME, I worked my way up from a criminal to a major. And now you guys have promoted me to Colonel with my own ship.

"I've had eight months to get used to being in the Alliance," McCloud continued. "The Alliance is where I dreamed of being, but it still feels weird. Back in the UME, even though I was a major, the general on Mars could have whipped out his sidearm and shot me down if I did something wrong. I wasn't a full-fledged major. I was the last of the London Proper scum. I had no rights. But here I no longer have to worry. I may get court-martialed if I do something wrong, but I won't just be gunned down. It's a nice feeling."

"So, what are you naming the ship?" I asked, trying to move back to more pleasant topics.

"I've known that since I was informed of my command. Since I represent the cabal and this ship was provided by the cabal, I'm going to name her *Caledonia.* She embodies the dream that one day Scotland will be free again. Man, is she a great ship, too. You guys have sure fixed her up nicely. One of the snipes told me she can do K-6. Can you believe that? K-6? I didn't know that was physically possible."

"Tell me about it," I agreed with him. "Richard says that he's even rigged the *Starwarden* to push K-7. That means going from Earth to Branson in under ten minutes. When I battled over Branson, my earth reinforcements were half an hour away."

"Things are different on this side," McCloud said. "The war is real. Isn't it?

"Yeah, McCloud. The war is very real here. Many have died already."

"The UME builds lots of ships, but they don't act like they're on a full war footing."

"They're outnumbered and outgunned," I said. "They know they can't win, while we're pushing ourselves toward assured victory."

"Unless they have alien tech we don't know about, sir."

"McCloud, don't call me sir. You're a colonel. That's O-6, same as a naval captain."

"Maybe," McCloud said, "but you're always going to be squad leader to me."

"The others have stopped thinking of me as their squad leader," I said.

"The others have had a couple years to readjust."

"True. I'm sorry I didn't come back for you guys."

"Don't be, Almek. I've told you before. London Proper was destroyed before you could possibly have come back."

"Then I just shouldn't have left anyone behind," I said.

"Almek, cut the crap," McCloud said. "You did what you had to do. You fought for a dream. Just like the cabal. In fact, just like me. My cabal colleagues are in grave danger, but I was the right one to leave."

We sat in silence for a while. Then I checked my implant and saw that we only had a handful of minutes before the christening. I was getting ready to tell McCloud it was time to go when he spoke.

"So, when are you going to marry her?"

"W…what?" I asked, completely thrown off by McCloud's new topic.

"You're what? Twenty…twenty-one now. During wartime, people always marry young, and twenty isn't that young anyway. Why don't you marry her?"

"To be honest, McCloud," I said. "I haven't even thought about it much. Running a ship keeps your mind going at least K-7. Maybe you're right, though. It would be nice."

"You should ask her. Seriously, this is war, you can use some joy in your life. There isn't anything like being married."

"What do you mean, McCloud? You aren't married."

"Actually, I am. I got married back in London Proper, during the Three Months' War. We never had time for a honeymoon. We finished the ceremony, and then we had to do a raid. It was still nice just to know that she was my wife. That we could at least be happy just because we were married. Then she was killed while on watch. I thought my life ended when she died, but I picked up the pieces when I joined the cabal. I fight to destroy the UME and revenge the death of my wife, Kathy McCloud.

"Think about it," McCloud continued. "War is rough, and it's nice to have a wife at your side. From what I've heard, Lauren is a great gal."

"She is, but hold on a second. You married Kathy?"

"Yeah," George said, a faint and longing smile on his face. "I miss her so much."

"When did this happen?" I asked. I couldn't absorb it. It was just so random.

"I already told you. It was during the Three Months' War."

"Man, McCloud. I really am sorry I didn't come and save you."

"Almek, marry Lauren before someone else does, or before one of you die. Or before the Draconians or the Garm destroy all of humanity. Maybe one of the UME monarchs takes a pot shot at you, your shields are down, and it goes straight through the captain's chair. You may not think it's likely, but it could happen."

"Thanks," I said. "You've got to give your speech in two minutes. We better get going. You do have the right opening statement?"

"Yeah," McCloud said. "I watched your speech, I won't forget the Passerines. They're going to be half of my crew."

"Good. Let's get going then."

***

"I am more accustomed to action than speech, so please bear with my lack of skill in speaking. Even something as simple as that phrase shows how well we have integrated with other species here in the Alliance. The first time I saw a Passerine, I was scared to death. They were just so different from us. Yet we have learned to become good friends with them. I've been selected as the skipper for this new ship, because I am a member of the Caledonian Cabal. I am honored to be given this command. Especially since we all hope that within the next six months or so there will be no need for a cabal. The UME should be long gone. Though the cabal may be gone by then, I won't be. I will stay with the Dalton Space Force. I hope that the rest of the cabal will likewise join the FSA. We will need all the might we can muster to destroy the Draconians after we have dealt with the UME.

"I promise that I will dedicate myself to my ship and crew. I am not just being placed here as a gesture. I have studied the ship hard for several months. I am as ready as anyone to take command. I hope that you will bear with me as I take command of this new ship that represents the dreams of Caledonia and of the entire Alliance."

Similar to the christening of the *Starwarden,* I watched the wall behind McCloud become transparent, and we could see the upgraded Monarch. Her hull, that had once been painted in the red and gold of the UME was now painted in the black of the Space Force, and at the bow of the ship was a large green outline of Scotland.

"I, Lieutenant Megan Kelso of the Caledonian Cabal, christen you in the name of the Four Species Alliance, as the Four Species Alliance Ship *Caledonia*!" She flung a bottle of Scotch at the ship.

"Oorah!" Sergeant Delgetty yelled. "Let's blast the UME!"

And the party commenced. I had only two goals. The first was to congratulate McCloud and the second was to find Lauren.

However, I never did accomplish the first goal. McCloud was nowhere to be found. Even his implant was offline, but I was soon distracted from McCloud's disappearance by finding Lauren. After six long months, we were finally together again. However, I couldn't enjoy the time we spent together as much as I hoped, because McCloud's advice kept echoing through my mind.

Chapter 11
Old Friends Reunite

Almek, McCloud called out over his implant, just as Lauren and I found an open table to sit down.

Your implant was offline. What's up?

I've got something that you have to come see. You won't believe it.

Where? I asked, curious, but also annoyed that my time with Lauren was being interrupted.

On the Free Trader Ellis. *Kai's in a SAP waiting for you. You'd better get here fast!*

"Well, Lauren," I said, sighing and standing up.

"I just got the message, too," she said. "Duty calls."

I helped her up, and we strolled to the SAP bay. However, when we arrived at the SAP bay, we were by no means alone. Jenny, Annabeth, and even the Sky Marshal were also there.

"Just what is this?" the Sky Marshal asked, as we got into Kai's SAP.

"I can't tell you, sir," Kai said. "You'll just have to be patient."

Like the Sky Marshal could ever be patient, I said to Kai.

"Can you at least give us a hint?" Jenny prodded.

"Fine," Kai said, turning around to face his passengers. "You are in for the shock of a lifetime."

I threw my hands in the air. "That's a lot of help!"

Kai docked with the guitar-shaped Free Trader *Ellis* and opened the airlock for us.

"Wait up," he said. "I wouldn't miss the looks on your faces for a fleet of Tomcats."

Kai led us through the empty corridors of the *Ellis* until we arrived at the cargo bay hatch. He held his hand over the keypad.

"Brace yourselves." He punched in a code, and the hatch dilated open.

The shock of a lifetime didn't do it justice. I couldn't believe what I was seeing at first and thought it had to be the most disgusting practical joke ever. My eyes jumped from face to face as I used my implant to scan many of my squad mates from London Proper. The thermal display confirmed that each of the images I looked at really were people. The implant confirmed that it wasn't an elaborate hologram, but I couldn't believe it.

Only after I'd scanned half of the room did I realize that Jack Dalton and High Alpha Sonnel were standing beside me.

"This will take a fair bit of explaining," Sonnel said, "but rest assured that they are all very real. Go ahead and greet them, and then Jack and I will explain everything."

"Sonnel," I said, on the verge of demanding an immediate explanation.

Just then, McCloud stepped out of the crowd, arm in arm with none other than Kathy and announced, "I'd like to introduce you to my wife, Kathy McCloud."

Both of them were grinning broadly, looking happier then I'd ever seen either of them before.

"It's good to see you again, Kathy," I said. "I am truly sor…"

"Oh, shut up, Almek," Kathy said. "Don't go there. Others fulfilled your promise for you, but I still consider it fulfilled, so don't say a word about it."

"Yes, ma'am," I said softly. Then I noticed a small DSF patch on her t-shirt. "You're in the Force?"

"Yeah," she said. "You almost caught me on Branson a couple years ago. I was really worried the cover for the operation would be blown before my husband could be rescued."

"That *was* you! And all my friends thought that I was losing it!"

"Yeah, it was me. And that was a good friend of mine you ended up grabbing, too. We had a good laugh about it after I recovered from the scare you gave me."

"I'll get you back for that, I promise."

"I'm sure you will."

"Look," I said. "I've got to greet everyone."

By the way, Kathy said. *I agree with George. You should marry her. She's perfect for you.*

I didn't respond to Kathy's comment, but instead went to greet my old squad. It seemed like just another night after a battle in London Proper. I greeted every member of my squad, and we talked about their career choices. Most of them were in the Force, but a few had chosen civilian jobs. Lauren felt out of place among the crowd, since she was surrounded by a roomful of strangers who all knew each other intimately. She stayed by my side and helped make one of the most important moments of my life perfect. After a couple hours, I had talked to everyone, and I found Jack Dalton again which he was deep in conversation with Jade.

"Do you mind if I steal Jack?" I asked Jade.

"Of course," Jade said. "He does seem to have quite a bit of explaining to do."

"Yes, he does."

"Well," Jack said, standing up. "Let's find Sonnel."

Before the words had even left his mouth, Sonnel was at his side. "You ready?" she asked me.

"Yes."

"Well, you know that I was personally watching over you and your squad while I lived with you disguised as Saph," Sonnel said.

"Yes, you told me that when I first met you."

"*I* helped you a lot in your battles against the other gangs in London."

"Yeah."

"When you were finally ready to leave London Proper, I called in backup. I hate saying this, but did you really think that a few kids with homemade weapons could steal a top-of-the-line UME naval ship?"

"I guess since we succeeded, I assumed that we could."

"Well, you didn't. I had called down most of the crew from the *Zochtil* to help you guys. We kept most of the marines busy elsewhere, which allowed your team to sneak in and steal the ship. We did the best that we could, but even with my team's tech, it was a tough operation and your squad suffered more casualties than we had expected. And, unfortunately, we couldn't breach the White House defenses, which is why your marine friends had to step in."

"Okay," I said, trying desperately to process all the information I'd been fed. It felt like my universe had been proven to be a big farce. "What about the people McCloud told me had died after our escape?"

"Once you left, we began evacuation immediately. We weren't able to save everyone, even though we had some expert help with the evacuation."

"This is where I got involved," Jack said. "When Sonnel first told me about you, I immediately took interest in you, as you obviously noticed. Any enemy of O'Brien is a friend of mine. I also figured that kids who had survived what you and your squad had been through had the mettle to be great assets, and I believed that some of them would want to join the war effort. Sonnel told me that she could evacuate your squad mates, but she didn't know what to do with them. So, I told her that I'd rescue them with Blue Squad, figuring that would be less of a shock for your squad mates. I offered shelter to each of them on Dalton Spaceways to allow them to recuperate until they were ready to find a permanent home. Blue Squad immediately started making rescue raids. We rescued as many as we could, but even with Canid tech, it was hard to avoid detection by the UME, because they were crawling all around London Proper. We did the best we could and found homes for your squad in DSI, the Space Force, or on Earth."

I sat in silence for a moment, still trying desperately to take it all in.

Lauren, however, wasn't in as much shock as I was and asked the most obvious question. "Why didn't you tell Almek? He's been fretting for years about how to get his friends out of London Proper, but he couldn't figure out how to do it."

"Well," Jack said, "we were still trying to figure out how to spring your squad mates from the UME. We kept the operation as secret as possible, figuring that if the UME discovered we had rescued the others, it would jeopardize the remainder of Operation Crown Jewel. But then McCloud solved that problem before we could."

"Wait a second," I said, as the pieces were still fitting into place. "What did the Sky Marshal know?"

"The Sky Marshal knew that his satellite scans showed London Proper being destroyed by the UME. He did nothing to help your friends."

"However," Sonnel said, "he didn't have the resources to help, and we did."

"Thanks," I said weakly. "I owe you guys so much."

"You helped save Colony One. I had billions invested there. Your debt is paid."

"You've helped the Canids, too," Sonnel said. "We've each helped the other when we could. We were glad we to extend a hand of friendship."

"Thanks," I said again.

Lauren led me to a table, and we sat down. After I was seated, it finally hit me. My friends were really alive! A massive wave of joy swept over me, and I started crying. Life was great, I thought, as Kathy and McCloud came over to our table. We talked and enjoyed each other's company just like–maybe better than–the old times in London Proper. All good things come to an end, and we had ships to report to, and a war to fight. But at least we had each other again.

Chapter 12

The Underground

"Captain, CIC."

"CIC, this is the captain," I said, hitting the intercom. "What's up?"

"Sir, you're not going to believe this," Ensign Taggart said. "I've got a Long-Range Tornado on my scanners."

"I believe you, Kris. I'm happy to hear that. I'll be on the bridge in a couple minutes."

"Understood, Captain."

Colonel McCloud.

Yeah, Almek? he asked.

I just got a report from CIC. We have a Long-Range Tornado on scan. I said.

This is the best news we've had in months. Do you want me to talk with them? McCloud asked.

Yes. Bring them in by the book, even though they're almost certainly allies.

Will do. I'll keep you updated.

"Captain's on the bridge," the BM of the watch said.

"At ease."

"CIC, this is the captain."

"CIC, here."

"CIC, I want you to contact Jade. I need you guys to try and plot that Tornado's previous course. I want to know where it came from. Got it?"

"Will do, sir."

"Good."

"Sir," a petty officer at comms said, "I've got an incoming message from Admiral Smith."

"Put him on my holo."

"Captain Manning," he said.

"Admiral."

"Do you have the situation under control?"

"Yes, sir," I replied. "We believe this is another message from the cabal. We were hoping they would try to make contact again. It looks like they decided to risk it. I'll keep you informed of the status."

"Thank you, Almek," Admiral Smith said. "Good luck."

"Sir," Emily said, as she took over the comm station. "*Caledonia* is patching us into an open channel with the tornado."

"This is Colonel George McCloud of the Four Species Alliance Ship *Caledonia*, identify yourself."

"This is Special Agent Henderson of G2. Is that really you, McCloud?"

"It sure is. You're really G2?"

"Yes, sir. From Titan."

"Good, we've been hoping G2 would send someone our way."

"McCloud, I need to speak to whoever is in command of your ship."

"I am, Henderson," McCloud said. I could hear the grin in his voice.

"They gave you a ship?"

"Yep. I'm the official G2 liaison for the FSA. Before we go any further though, you need to give me the codes."

"Of course," Henderson said. He proceeded to provide the password for McCloud's op, which had only been known only by his cell and by McCloud's general.

"That is correct," McCloud said. "You may continue."

"So, the Solar Fleet has finally accepted us?" Henderson continued the previous conversation. "That is awesome. I need to speak to the Sky Marshal or someone high up. G2's got plans and if the Solar Fleet …"

"It's the Four Species Alliance," McCloud said. "The Solar Fleet is only a small part of this."

"Even better, but G2 has plans, and the Four Species Alliance should help. We're ready to revolt. It's time for the revolution," Henderson said. "We're going to take back our homeland."

"Okay," McCloud said. "This whole conversation was patched in to the Big Three. I'm sure they can't wait to talk to you in person. I've got a wing of Passerine fighters headed your way, along with a tug. We'll bring you into the cargo bay. How copy?"

"Good copy, sir," Henderson said.

"Marines," I heard the OOD mutter to the right of me. "Good copy? We're in the Fleet up here."

"Yeah, but old habits die hard, and technically McCloud is still a marine," I said in defense of my friend

"True, sir."

"Emily," I said, turning to my comm officer. "I want a secure link with the Sky Marshal."

"Will do."

"Sky Marshal, did you get all of that?" I said over the comm link.

"Yes, I did. I've got the *Sky* en route to Colony One right now. Don't start the meeting without me."

"Don't worry, we won't. Just don't make us wait too long. And, remember, it's not Colony One, it's Branson."

"Old habits," the Sky Marshal said. "See you shortly."

***

It seemed that I just kept finding myself at these meetings with the Big Three, because here I was again with the Sky Marshal, Jack Dalton, High Admiral Numair, Sonnel, George McCloud, Admiral Smith, Agent Henderson, and our respective staffs.

"Colonel-Skipper McCloud says that we can trust you," Numair said.

"Yes," McCloud said. "He had the proper codes, and I interviewed him in depth. I'm certain that he is an ally."

"Good," the Sky Marshal said. "Then tell us what you came here for."

"The leaders of the cabal wish to speak to you in person." Henderson stopped there, as if that was his whole message.

"Don't you have anything else to say?" the Sky Marshal asked.

"I have details of how to arrange the meeting, but that is the message. The leaders of the cabal wish to speak to you in person. They have plans that you need to hear."

"What are these plans?" Jack asked before the Sky Marshal could speak again.

"I wasn't informed of them for obvious reasons," Henderson said. "I was just about the lowest-ranking member of the cabal on Titan. They didn't want to risk their plans falling into the wrong hands. However, I was given as much information as possible about McCloud and his men, so that I could convince you I was from the cabal if you didn't trust the codes."

The Sky Marshal turned to McCloud.

"As I said, sir," McCloud answered the unasked question. "I believe that he is from the cabal. He gave the codes perfectly, and I interviewed him while we waited for you to arrive. I stake my career on him being a legitimate member of the cabal."

"Okay," the Sky Marshal said. "How are we supposed to meet with the cabal leaders?"

"You will have to go to Titan."

"Wait a second," the Sky Marshal objected. "You want us to just land on a planet controlled by the UME?"

"No, sir," McCloud responded, answering for Henderson. "I believe I've mentioned this before. Titan is the headquarters of the cabal. At least half of the soldiers there are cabal members. They can swing this without the UME even knowing what happened."

"We don't want you to just stroll onto the planet," Henderson said. "The general believes that you have cloaking devices. Is this true?"

"Yes," Jack said, before the Sky Marshal could object to revealing classified information.

The Sky Marshal glared at Jack, but he didn't say anything.

"Good," Henderson said. "The cabal wants you to come in with your ships cloaked. I have a memory orb with the location and codes for the docking bay you'll land in. From there we have cabal members who will escort you to secret chambers of the cabal. You can talk, then leave the same way you came in."

"Sounds too simple," Jessica Dale muttered from behind me.

I nodded in agreement, as I watched the Big Three.

"We can't all go in," Jack was the first to speak. "I volunteer."

"You already went on the mission to the Passerines," the Sky Marshal said.

"Exactly," Jack said. "I'm the better diplomat. I'll go. I'll also take Almek, McCloud, and Blue Squadron. We'll go in one of our joint spec ops boarding shuttles."

"We'll want a fighter escort, too," I said.

"Fighters are too small for a cloaking device," the Sky Marshal said.

"That's not true," Jack said. "There's one fighter that has a cloaking device."

"Captain Shey Hunter's customized fighter," I supplied the data. "She's a quintuple ace. Best pilot in the Alliance."

"Okay," the Sky Marshal said. "It sounds like we have a plan, except that you'll take Bronski's STAR team, instead of Blue Squadron. We need some Solar Fleet personnel there. When are we supposed to meet them?"

"In one week," Henderson said. "The exact time is on the orb."

***

Commodore Hunter, I linked with her. I *need to speak with you in my stateroom.*

Wilco, Captain. Shey said. *I'll be there in fifteen minutes. I'm in the middle of a sim with my team.*

Okay, fifteen minutes.

Ending link, sir.

I waited for fifteen minutes, thinking about the past year I'd spent with Shey as my CAG. After the battle in which we rescued the *Caledonia,* Shey had been very civil towards me. She hadn't gotten into any trouble recently, and I was beginning to think that she might have calmed down and cooled off. She was becoming an essential and important part of my crew. I also thought that her fighter squads respected her more, now that they had seen her in action. I still wasn't quite sure how she felt about her assignment on the *Starwarden,* though.

"Commodore Shey Hunter reporting as ordered, sir."

"Please have a seat, Shey," I said, gesturing towards an open chair. "Do you like serving on this ship, Commodore?" I asked her, going straight to my point of concern.

"Originally, no, sir. I didn't like you. I thought you were young and stuck up."

"Interesting, Shey," I said. "I thought the same thing about you. How old are you?"

"Twenty-two, sir."

"I'm twenty."

"Yes, sir," Shey said. "However, after the battle, I've formed a better working relationship with my pilots. I've also learned to work with you as my CO. I did a lot of stupid things when I first came aboard. This crew doesn't tolerate stunts, and neither do you. You've got the best crew in the Alliance on this ship. I don't want to mess that up by being a stuck-open damper grill in your reactor core."

"Thank you. So you're happy on the *Starwarden* now?" I asked.

"Yes, sir, I'd say so," she said.

"Shey," I interrupted her. "I expect the sirs when we're in public, but in private we share the same rank. I'm still your commanding officer, but call me Almek or Captain, not sir."

"Wilco," she said with a smile. "As I was saying, I'm happy here. This is a great ship. I feel more at home here than I have anywhere else. In fact, this is the first ship I've considered home. The *Starwarden* is my home, sir. I love it here."

"That's quite a turnaround," I said.

"Almek, I've fought alongside my pilots, and I've fought with you watching our six. We're family now."

"Shey," I said. "Jack…, I mean Mr. Dalton, said that you have always been a trouble-maker aboard ship. Why the turnaround? You've fought with other pilots before."

"Commodore Drove had already set up a superb integrated fighter wing. I inherited his work, which I now see was better than anything I had done before. And these pilots watch each other's back like no group I've seen before. No recriminations, no blame, just total loyalty. And I almost lost it before I recognized what I had. This is home now. You won't get any more trouble from me unless you try to reassign me."

"Good," I said. "I wanted to make sure that was settled. And, now, I've got a crucial mission I need you to perform."

"What is it?"

"We're going to meet with the leaders of the cabal on Titan."

"On Titan, sir?"

"Yes, the Big Three have committed to this mission. We'll go in dark, fully cloaked, and we want you as our fighter escort."

"What are you going down in?" she asked.

"A boarding shuttle."

"Okay, that makes sense. I would love to escort you guys in, but this mission could go south quickly, and one fighter isn't much."

"One fighter is all we can bring. Plus it is being piloted by a quintuple ace?"

"I may be good, but I'm not god. That's your job."

"Thanks for the reminder," I said sardonically. I had never liked the common naval analogy of a ship captain to that of a god.

"Any time, Almek. I have to shoot down overblown aviator egos all the time. I'm used to it."

"I'm sure you are, dismissed."

She was just headed out the door when I called out to her again. "Shey."

"Yes, Almek," she said, turning to face me.

"Welcome to the *Starwarden*."

She smiled. "Thanks."

***

"We're in orbit about Ganymede," Jessica said. "You're cleared for departure."

"Understood," Ed said, from the pilot's station of the spec ops boarding shuttle.

We had left the two tugs that were normally in our shuttle bay back at Branson's Spacedock so we could fit one of the spec ops boarding ships inside. On a normal mission, they would have simply docked to one of the five spaces built on the hull of the *Starwarden* designed specifically for the spec ops ships. However, that wouldn't work on this mission. The boarding shuttle couldn't cloak while attached to the ship.

"This is Commodore Hunter," Shey said. "I'm in position. We're ready to go. Cloaking device is on." Shey was our sole lookout and had exited before us so she could cover us all on the way in.

"Roger," Ed said. "Lifting landing gear ... cloaking. We're cloaked. Exiting the shuttle bay now."

I watched us leave the shuttle bay from my implant, which was linked to a camera on top of the boarding ship. It was a tight squeeze, and I couldn't help but flinch as we passed within half a meter of the shuttle bay doors.

"That was close," I muttered.

"Are you doubting my pilot's skill?" Bronski asked, smiling at me.

"Of course not," I said. "It's still scary. I trusted Jade when we did a 180 degree turn at K-5, but I was still scared to death."

"I never would have guessed that the great Almek Manning could be scared."

I turned to face the Passerine admiral who had made that comment.

"Admiral Slumnar," I said, "why do you keep patronizing me?

"I'm simply not convinced you really are all that High Admiral Numair says you are."

Okay, team, Bronski linked, taking control of the op. *We're heading in to Titan. Try to stay close to us Shey, but just don't ram us. So hold tight, this is going to be a long couple of hours.*

Aye, aye, Shey replied.

***

"Ensign Connaley," Bronski said. "Open up a secure tight-beam channel with the coordinates that G2 provided."

She instinctively turned to me to make sure I agreed. I nodded. "This is Bronski's ship, not mine."

"Will do," she said sheepishly. We waited five minutes. "It's open. You're on."

"G2, this is Jack Dalton," Jack said, "representing the Four Species Alliance. Do we have clearance to land?"

"Mr. Dalton," a voice responded, "you may land, but stay cloaked."

"Acknowledged," Jack said.

"The connection was already closed," Emily said.

"Well then," Bronski said, "Ed, take her down. Emily, inform Shey we're going down. She's to follow us."

"Understood," Emily said.

"Here we go," Ed said. "Entering atmo now."

"Gear up!" Bronski ordered. "We need to be ready to go in five. I want everyone in battle gear and armed to the teeth, or wing tips, as the case may be."

I got into a combat suit, grabbed the SCAR that Scourge handed me, and took my position at the door, behind Tobias. Scourge and Bronski took the other side. Only Jack Dalton refused to get into combat gear. He had a sidearm strapped to his jeans and his t-shirt read: "Branson – Humanity's First Home Outside Sol System."

"We've landed," Ed said. He didn't shut down any of the ship's systems. He just turned off the cloaking device, but kept the shuttle primed for launch. "We're ready to go at your command, boss."

"Thanks," Bronski acknowledged. "Emily?"

"Shey isn't responding, sir."

"Were there any explosions?" I asked, letting go of my rifle, which instantly snapped to my side as the shoulder strap tightened.

"No, sir," Ed said. "I didn't see any."

This is Commodore Hunter, Shey linked. *I've landed. Requesting orders.*

Stay put, Bronski said.

You gave us quite the scare, I told her.

Don't try to open a channel with me when I'm trying to land in a new hangar.

We're going to take this one nice and slow, Bronski said, interrupting our conversation. *Everybody switch to outside camera view. Cycle between cameras. I want to know the second someone shows up to greet us.*

"Sir," Ed said. "Sensors are detecting autoguns. I'm picking up at least five aimed at the shuttle."

"Can you jam them?" Bronski asked.

"Working on it," Thomas said, as he moved away from the door and to his console.

"I see the welcoming party," I told him. "Camera three."

"I see 'em," Bronski said. "Open the doors, Ed."

Chapter 13

More Allies

"Okay, team," Bronski said, "let's get this docking bay secured."

Bronski, Scourge, and I exited the shuttle. I looked up and saw the doors overhead irising shut. We were secure. Nobody who wasn't supposed to know about us would be able to spot us. However, it would also be harder to get back out.

Bronski took up a position on one of the wings, down on one knee, with his own handcrafted rifle aimed at the welcoming committee. Scourge took up the same stance on the other wing. I walked out to meet the greeting party.

"I'm Captain Almek Manning," I said. I held tightly onto my rifle, but it was close to my chest, pointing down in a non-threatening fashion. "I hope you excuse the other men," I waved at Bronski and Scourge. "They're spec ops. Best team in the Alliance."

"Not a problem," the man wearing three stars said. "I'm Admiral MacGregor of G2."

At this point, Jack Dalton walked out of the darkened interior of the shuttle with Admiral Slumnar at his side.

Sirs, Thomas linked. *I've got control of the autoguns and the docking bay iris. We can leave whenever you want.*

Thanks, Thomas, Bronski replied. *I knew I could count on you. Now get out here with us. Ed, report.*

Engines hot. We can go whenever.

Emily, Bronski said. *Tell Shey she can come out now. You can come down if you want.*

I'll stick to the ship, but I'll inform Shey, Emily responded.

"This is Jack Dalton owner of Dalton Space Industries and Dalton Space Force," I said, motioning toward Jack. Just then, Shey appeared a few meters from the shuttle. The cabal soldiers tensed up instantly. Bronski and Scourge hadn't fazed them, but a fighter appearing out of nowhere had obviously startled them.

"Lower your weapons!" Bronski shouted, raising his own and aiming it at one of the soldiers.

"Lower your weapons," Admiral MacGregor ordered. "It's just their escort fighter."

The men slowly lowered their weapons, but they watched Shey carefully as she walked toward me, her own SCAR slung across her back, helmet tucked under her arm.

"And," I said, continuing the introductions, "this is Admiral Slumnar of the Passerines."

I watched the cabal soldiers eye the alien warily. They obviously hadn't been around aliens. However, MacGregor didn't seem surprised by the alien presence.

"It's good to see we have allies," he said simply.

"You do not have allies," Slumnar said. "I serve the Four Species Alliance. The Caledonian Cabal is not an official member."

"Too true," MacGregor said. "Can we go to our conference room, so we can hold discussions in a civilized fashion?"

"I'm not comfortable with that, sir," Bronski said, his rifle still aimed at the cabal members. I wondered why he had said that out loud instead of over the implant.

"That is why you're a captain, and I own a multi-trillion credit company," Jack said. *I'm the diplomat, Bronski. I'm making the decisions. You just provide maximum security after I've decided what to do. Understood?*

Sir, yes, sir, Bronski linked.

Good. Jack said. "Let's go. Please excuse my security detail."

"No problem," MacGregor said. "This way."

The admiral led us inside, and I turned back to see Emily take up a sniping position on top of the shuttle, although I was pretty sure everyone could tell firearms weren't her specialty. I smiled when I noticed she was still wearing her chaplain insignia.

Bronski and Scourge were following behind us, watching for

trouble, and it looked like they were hoping they would find some. We were led through a maze of tunnels but, if G2 was trying to get us lost, they would fail. I had my implant recording the path back to the shuttle, and the others would all be doing the same.

Finally, we reached a conference room. Bronski and Scourge stood outside the door along with a couple G2 guards, who didn't look happy to have a STAR team next to them. I walked into the room with Jack and Slumnar. There was a four-star general in the room already, but that was it.

"Is this the entire conference?" Jack asked.

"Yes," the general said. "We didn't want to overwhelm you by having too many of us here."

"General, after having negotiated a treaty on an alien planet where the nearest human was light years away, my threshold for being overwhelmed is a little higher then this."

"I knew you were allied with aliens even before you came here," the general said.

"How did you know?" Jack asked.

"I guess there's something you should see before we start the discussion," the general said. He stood up, giving me a chance to read the name O'Leary on his nameplate.

"Okay, lead the way," Jack said, getting up. *Bronski, Scourge, you may enter. We're headed out.*

Bronski and Scourge came through the door with the G2 guards at their heels.

"Sir," a G2 guard called out, "they just burst in."

"It's okay, we're leaving this room for a moment. Just stay here," O'Leary instructed.

We followed O'Leary through a side door and traversed more hallways until we found ourselves at a door guarded by sixteen men. They stiffened and formed up, aiming their guns at Slumnar.

"General," one of the guards said, addressing O'Leary. "Are you being held captive?"

"No. These are all friends. Let us through."

They hesitated, but eventually formed up on either side of the hallway. I could feel the tension in Bronski's body as we passed through the cabal's ranks. We entered the room and found a small device in the center of an otherwise empty room, and, next to the device, we saw a tablet. We walked up to the device.

Admiral Slumnar swore under his breath. "That's an artifact of the Ancient Enemy!" he said.

"And we know how to use it," the general said. "Don't worry, we have not found any aliens, just their technology."

Just? Jack said. *Just their technology. Not much then.*

"This device has insane computing power," MacGregor said, stepping up to the device and picking up the tablet. "It can link into almost any network and strip the data from it. We've been able to reverse engineer some of this technology and now can hack into almost any communication channel without needing to use this device. It has pulled intel from every database we could link it to. But don't worry," he said, turning to look at Jack. "You'll be happy to know that we were never successfully hacked into the DSI database."

Jack nodded. "That would probably be the hack we detected and blocked the month before I left to negotiate with the Passerines."

"This device has kept me pretty well informed about the Solar Fleet, even if didn't give me a direct pipe to DSI," MacGregor said. "I haven't shared this with the UME. My team wrote the programs, and only G2 knows about it. So, I knew you were allied with at least one alien species, that you had extra-solar colonies before the blockade was breached, and much more."

"What other alien tech does the UME have?" Slumnar asked.

"A lot," O'Leary replied. He handed Jack a memory orb. "This contains specs of the alien tech I have clearance to know about, which I hope is most of it."

"Can I just have an idea of how much tech the UME has

managed to reverse engineer?" Jack asked.

"A lot," O'Leary repeated, "but most of it doesn't have military significance. And there's much more that we still don't understand. Look at this." O'Leary typed in a couple commands and stepped back. A hologram shot out from the device and lit up the room. It was a hologram of a ship that appeared to be about twenty times larger than the *Starwarden* based on the visual cues embedded in the holographic image.

"This ship," MacGregor began. "Is still on Mars. It is buried in a long disguised hangar that we just recently discovered. The UME is working on getting this ship up and running. If they do, the Solar Fleet …"

"Four Species Alliance," Slumnar corrected.

"The Four Species Alliance won't have a chance. We have to act now."

"Just how powerful is this ship?" I asked.

"That's the problem," O'Leary said. "We don't have any idea, but just look at this."

O'Leary zoomed in on a relatively small section of the ship. The object filling the screen appeared to be a cannon of some kind. O'Leary superimposed another image over the weapon. The image was that of a Heinlein class fast cruiser carrier, and it was barely larger than the cannon.

"Does that answer your question sufficiently?"

"All too well," I said.

"So what is your plan?" Jack asked, his gaze still fixed on the massive weapon.

"Let's go back to the conference room first," O'Leary said.

We hiked back to the conference room, while my mind turned over the concept of this new ship. The Alliance clearly had to get this ship before the UME figured out how to use it.

"Okay," O'Leary said, as he sat down on a chair in the conference room, "we strike in four months. We can take Titan almost bloodlessly, and we have people in key spots on Mars that will make even Mars be a relatively easy target. We have personnel placed where they can overload the cores of their ships. The UME shouldn't have that ship up and running for at least another six months to a year, but the sooner we strike the better. We can't risk letting them get the jump on us."

"Logical," Jack said. "Besides intel and Titan is there anything else you guys can provide to us?"

"Not really," O'Leary said. "We don't have much else to give. We have a couple of teams here who could assist on the ground, but they wouldn't increase your numbers by much."

"Well," Jack said. "The truth is that if we believe you actually are a cabal, you're in the Alliance for sure. I believe you're legitimate. So, welcome to the Four Species Alliance."

"Thanks," O'Leary said, with obvious relief. He put out his hand, and they shook on the Alliance. "I'm glad to be part of something larger than the cabal."

"No problem," Jack said, "but we'll need to be able to communicate to plan an attack. Can your hackers pick up our implant calls?"

"Your what?" MacGregor asked.

"Our cranial implants," Jack said, tapping his forehead.

"Here," I said. "I'll call Jack. See if you can pick it up."

Opening Link, Jack said.

We started quoting books to each other just to keep the conversation going, while MacGregor called his control room. After ten minutes, MacGregor shook his head.

"I can't pick up anything."

"Good," Jack said. "If you come to Manning's ship, I could have both you and O'Leary outfitted with implants. That way we could communicate with you all the time."

"That sounds great," MacGregor said.

O'Leary seemed a little more hesitant, but he also agreed.

"Well, then, let's go," I said. I was eager to be back in space.

"I'll lead the way," MacGregor said, as we walked out through the main door.

"That's okay," Bronski said. "I can handle it."

MacGregor watched in awe as Bronski led us through the winding corridors and back to the hangar where the boarding shuttle was docked. Once we were all aboard, Ed took us up.

"Give me a second to open up the doors," MacGregor said.

"It's already done," Thomas replied, smugly

MacGregor stared at Thomas. "Is there anything these guys can't do?" he asked us.

"No," I said. "They're the best. They've captured two Draconian ships. Overriding a simple computer isn't hard for them."

MacGregor shook his head in astonishment. "Well, I guess they'll be the perfect candidates for capturing that alien warship."

"We're the only candidates," Bronski said.

"Just a tad cocky?" O'Leary asked.

"No," Bronski said with a grin, "just trying to make sure nobody gets any ideas about giving another team a cut of *our* action."

Chapter 14
Two-Pronged Attack

Three months later, I was in yet another meeting with the top brass. Our Zarc ambassador had just come in for another brief visit, and we were ready to confront him about all the UME's Phobian technology.

"Well," the Sky Marshal said, standing up once we had all arrived. "Let's get to the most important item first." The Sky Marshal pressed a few controls, and the hologram of the Phobian ship appeared in the center of the table.

A very strange noise came out of the cloud that was the Zarc ambassador. I could only assume it was the Zarc equivalent of gasping.

"Where did you get this image?" the ambassador demanded, as the cloud grew larger.

"We received this from spies within the UME," the Sky Marshal responded. "The UME found this in a hangar far beneath the surface of Mars, the planet that the Phobians never inhabited. They've found many other technological remnants on the planet. We need to know what we could face when we attack Mars."

"What else do you know?"

I used my tablet to pull up a chemical model holo of the poisonous gas that Lee had used on Bronski and his team.

"No, not that," the Zarc said, gasping again. "I must go!"

"Whoa!" the Sky Marshal ordered. "I've still got questions for you."

But he was too late. The Zarc had vanished again, and his ship departed seconds after.

"Well, there goes that plan," Jack said. "I guess we'll be winging it on this mission."

"Looks like," the Sky Marshal said. "We'll be attacking both

Mars and the UME defenses on Earth at the same time. SF Strike Groups One and Two will attack Mars. DSF Assault Force Alpha and the Passerine Earth Defense Fleet will attack earth with the support of the DSF orbitals and the *Zochtil*.

"The hardest part of this battle will be the marines' job," the Sky Marshal said.

"Oorah!" the four-star marine general exclaimed.

The Sky Marshal nodded. "The war on the ground will be tough. We don't have a clue what fortifications they have on Mars, and Earth is full of civs. I'll support the ground attack once we eliminate the threat from the stars. General Michaela Cestari will lead the ground assault on Mars, while General Hubbard will be leading the assault on Earth. I'd like to point out," the Sky Marshal said, turning to face Michaela, "that General Cestari has fulfilled all the requirements for Sky Marshal, so if I die during this mission, Michaela will take over."

"I don't intend to be taking that job from you any time soon, though," General Cestari said.

"I hope you don't," the Sky Marshal agreed. "Okay, we leave in two weeks. Let's finish this war!"

We all cheered. It was about time that we stopped fighting other humans and moved on to the much more powerful alien threat. After the meeting, I walked over to talk with Nicole.

"Nicole," I said, putting out my hand to shake.

"Grow up, Almek," Nicole said, bringing me in for a short hug. "It's great to see you again."

"Same. How was boot camp?"

"A lot rougher than naval boot camp," Nicole said, smiling. "But you'll be able to get through it."

"What?" I said, stepping back a pace and looking at her sharply. "What are you talking about?"

"After me, you're next in line. I'm betting after we beat the UME, the Sky Marshal will send you off to boot camp."

"I decided a long time ago I was perfectly happy with stopping at captain. I have no desire to be Sky Marshal."

"Yes," Nicole said. "That may be true, but you've never shirked your duty before. If called upon, would you refuse?"

"I don't know," I said honestly. "I may have other responsibilities when I'm called upon."

"Ah, so you've decided to ask Lauren then?"

"Why is it that everybody thinks I need to rush into marriage?"

"Because it's war," Jack Dalton said, on his way out of the conference room. "And you two are pretty well matched."

I threw my hands up in the air. "Okay! Okay! Let me handle my own relationships. Is it too much to ask?"

"If you're not being clueless," Nicole said, smiling. "Come on, I'll buy you lunch."

***

Thirty-six hours before we were to leave for Mars, I invited all of my squad to the *Starwarden* for a feast to relax, catch up, and enjoy each other's company. Chefo really went all out with the meal, and he had the officers' wardroom tables piled high with delicious food from all over the known universe. Lauren arrived early, and the two of us talked and laughed easily, as we hadn't seen each other outside of formal meetings for almost two months. George and Kathy joined the feast. Richard arrived with a cute gal from The Lab on his arm, and Nicole and Jenny arrived together. Even Bronski, Armistead, and Kai were able to join us. Once Kai showed up, Shey pulled him aside, and they started talking shop about the *Starwarden's* space wing. I had even talked Kris into coming. Then came the real surprise. Jade was the last to arrive, and on her arm was none other than Jack Dalton.

"Jade," I said. "Welcome. When did this happen?"

Jade smiled. "I've been dating Jack for quite some time. Since before we christened the *Caledonia*."

"How did we not know about this?" Jenny asked. "And what happened to Max?"

"Well, Max left the Fleet after the Battle of the Blockade. We tried to keep up a relationship, but it's hard enough having a boyfriend up here in space, while it's impossible with someone on Earth. You're probably just about the only ones who don't know about us, though. It's been all over the tabloids for months."

"You think a couple of ship captains have time to read the tabloids?" I asked.

"Well, I hope they aren't bugging you too much," Lauren said.

"As a gal from a small town in Kansas," Jade said, "I'm not used to anywhere near this kind of attention. I was put in the town paper when I got accepted into the Fleet, but that was as much publicity as I'd ever been subjected to."

"I do a pretty good job keeping them off station on the rare occasions you give Jade leave," Jack said, looking at me.

"You could always give me an order," I told him, smiling.

"I'm sure the Sky Marshal would approve of that," Jack said sarcastically.

"Well, I wouldn't mind," Jade said.

"I would. I need you here," I countered.

"Well, are y'all going to spend the whole time talkin', or can we dig into this feast," Arm said, greedily eyeing the food laid out on the table.

"I'm all for eating!" McCloud agreed.

Once I'd gotten my food, I made sure to sit next to the McClouds. I was dying to talk to Kathy some more. Lauren sat with me, and she and Kathy really hit it off. I found it hard to get a word in edgewise. So, finally, McCloud and I gave up and had our own conversation. After awhile, McCloud pulled me aside.

"So, was it your plan to ask Lauren now?"

"Whoa," I said. "We're going into battle in less than two days."

"Exactly," McCloud said. "We could have Emily perform the ceremony, or any of the many ship captains here, then you and Lauren would have about thirty-four hours before go time."

"Except that we both have responsibilities on our own ships."

"It could be arranged."

"Look," I said. "I don't have a ring, so drop it."

"What was that?" Lauren asked, as she sauntered over to us.

"McCloud was just asking me if I had bothered to get a class ring from the Academy," I quickly lied.

"I figured Almek would be proud to be a ring knocker," McCloud said with a grin.

"It's not that," I retorted. "The rings were just way too expensive. And, as the Force doesn't have traditional schooling, I wouldn't have felt right wearing one in the Force."

"Sure," McCloud said, winking at me.

***

"We will be in battle formation over Mars in five seconds," the helmsman called out. "Four, three, two, one. We are going at light, half-light. We're maintaining a steady point one of c towards the enemy formation."

"Sensors are warming up!" another watchstander yelled out.

"Bridge, CIC."

"CIC, this is the Bridge."

"Bridge, we've got twenty Monarchs plus their escorts."

"Understood," I said. "Commodore Hunter, launch the space wing."

"Roger that," Shey said. "Launching space wing. Let's show the UME that you can't mess with the FSA!"

"Hooyah!" I heard a fighter pilot yell out.

"Call off," Shey ordered. "Form up."

I switched off the aviator circuit. "CIC, target alpha-charlie-ten

125

with the phasic shield!"

"Target locked!"

"Fire antimatter torpedoes!"

I watched as two torpedoes flew at the ship. They hit the enemy Monarch, and we had one less ship to deal with.

"Lock on alpha-charlie-three!" I ordered.

"Phasic shield deflected!"

"What? Try again, CIC!"

"Trying…sir, I'm not getting a lock on anything larger than a frigate."

I swore. "They've obviously improved their tech."

I turned to my holodisplay to watch the battle, and suddenly a massive energy blast shot out from the surface.

"CIC, what was that?" I asked.

"Unsure, sir. It was an energy discharge of an unknown weapon class from Mars' surface."

"Did it hit anything?" asked Jade, who was acting as JOOD.

"Yes, ma'am. It completely knocked out two fighters. All of their systems are down, and negative response on implants."

"What was that?" I asked. "That was not in the database that G2 gave us."

"I'm running it again," Kris said from CIC. "I'm also running it past General O'Leary and Admiral MacGregor."

"I need answers fast!" I shouted.

"I'm running it."

"Good, take care of it," I said. I spun around to face the BM of the watch. "BM, try to locate the weapon firing those shots."

"Working on it, sir."

Opening link, Bronski said.

Bronski, prepare boarding shuttles for undock. Did you see the energy discharge?

Yes, sir.

We're trying to locate the weapon. I'll send your team down to destroy it. I want a plan, so be ready to go as soon as I give you the okay.

Will do, sir.

"Almek, this is the Sky Marshal."

"Roger."

"Did you see the discharge?"

"Yes, sir. I've got my BM of the watch locating it. CIC is trying to figure out what it is. I also have Bronski and the spec ops teams ready to go down and take it out."

"Good," the Sky Marshal said. "Make it hot for them!"

"Shey, update!" I called out.

"We're doing good, sir! I haven't lost any fighters yet, and we've taken down quite a few ships."

"CIC and Engineering," I said. "Do I have an update on the phasic shield?"

"Sir," Duval said. "We can't figure this one out. Nothing wrong on this end."

"I'm not getting a lock," CIC said.

"Richard," I said, switching channels to the torpedo bay.

"Septi-dimensional torps ready, sir."

"Good. Prepare them to be fired."

G2, this is the Sky Marshal! I heard the Sky Marshal call out over the implant.

G2 here.

Tell your men to overload the cores, and cause as much havoc as they can.

Will do, General O'Leary said. *They're ready. I'm sending the message now. Transmitting ship coordinates to you. Don't waste your weapons on them.*

Roger, I'm sending the list to the fleet now, the Sky Marshal said.

"Richard, I want one torpedo heading towards each of these three Monarchs." I highlighted three Monarchs on my display and sent the data on to Richard's crew in the torpedo bay.

I watched as Richard's ultra expensive torpedoes shot off into the distance. The Monarchs were phased out, but the torpedoes caught them, and soon there were three clouds of debris.

"Brilliant job, Richard!" I shouted. "I just wish we had hundreds of those."

"I've got a lock!" CIC shouted over the intercom.

"Fire three antimatter torpedoes!" Jessica shouted back. "Take that ship down!"

"Sirs, I've got more ships coming up from the surface."

"Shey," I ordered, "divert to the ships coming up from the surface. I don't want them joining the battle!"

"Wilco," she said. "Escorting the Condors and other bombers now. We'll take out those ships for you, sir."

"CIC and BM, I need an update on that discharge."

"CIC, here," Kris said. "I've got nothing on my end. It isn't in the database, and it didn't ring any bells with our contacts at G2."

"Roger," I acknowledged. "BM?"

"I think I've found it. One more second, sir. I've got its location!" he shouted. "I'm sending the coordinates to you now."

I pulled up the coordinates on my display and swore. I saw the massive dome and gun. It looked a lot like an ancient domed telescope. All around its sides were massive gun ports. I saw eight of them and quickly transmitted the data to Bronski.

"Jessica you have the bridge, I need to take care of this."

"Aye, sir."

Bronski, here's your target, I linked with Bronski.

Bronski swore too. *They sure do have it well guarded.*

Okay, I've got a couple options here, Bronski said. *Give me a second. I've got to run some sims.*

Okay. I impatiently waited for Bronski to get back to me.

I've got two options. Transmitting the sims.

I pulled them up and started to run the first one.

The first plan calls for us landing outside of the gun's range and going in on foot. Expected casualties are nil going down. Approximating twenty percent casualties once we're inside, though. Estimated time to destruction is fifteen to thirty minutes.

Unacceptable, I said. *We don't know how long it takes to charge, but its next shot might take out something larger than a couple fighters. We obviously can't afford having the* Starwarden *disabled.*

That was the best option, Bronski said. *Here's the second option.*

"Sir," Jessica called out. "I need your advice."

I looked up at the main holodisplay and saw we had two more Monarchs bearing down on us.

"Richard, put a torpedo through each of those Monarchs."

"Got it."

"Jessica," I said. "I'm working on a bigger problem. Next time ask Ardent."

"Yes, sir."

Continue Bronski, I ordered.

I started up the second sim while Bronski explained it to me. They would come in right over the target, with cloaking devices on. However, I watched the descent and saw one of the ship's cloaking device go down for just a couple seconds, but all eight gun fortifications turned on the shuttle and it exploded into more debris. Before the other ships made it to the ground, they lost two more shuttles the same way. I watched as even more of the men died exiting the shuttles to make an assault against the main cannon.

That was the best-case scenario, Bronski said. *The computer is saying we've got a thirty percent chance of losing all five shuttles on the way down.*

Fine. Go with the first plan, I said. *Just let me run it past the Sky Marshal. Prepare for undock.*

We're ready.

"Sky Marshal, this is Almek."

I quickly sent him the sims and told him the plan.

"Sounds good," he said. "Move out."

Go! Go! Go! I ordered Bronski.

The five spec ops boarding shuttles undocked and cloaked, and I assumed they started heading toward the surface.

"CIC," I asked. "How are shields holding up?"

"Maybe ten percent," they said.

"Boost power to the shields," I ordered.

Suddenly, the ship shook with multiple impacts.

I swore. "Jessica, I have the bridge. What was that?"

"I'm not sure," Jessica said.

"This is Duval. Almost all of the systems here in engineering flickered when we were hit. That's why you were able to feel the impact of the missiles."

"Why did it go through the shields?" I asked.

"This is CIC," Kris said. "I'm checking on it now. Here are the coordinates of the ship that fired those missiles."

"Richard, send out another special torp at the designated coordinates."

"Will do."

"Sir," Kris said. "My leading chief's got the data you wanted."

"Put him on."

"This is Senior Chief Lamar."

"Okay, what's the data?"

"The missile appears to be a standard UME missile, but it was enhanced with a phasing field of some sort. It is this field that allowed it to pass through our shields. They also appear to have an energy field. It's similar to an EMP, but not quite the same. Maybe an ionized missile would be the correct description. Anyway, the energy field was able to temporarily knock out our systems. We've lost a handful of primary systems and have been forced to patch in redundant control systems."

We were hit again by three more missiles.

"Where are those missiles coming from?" I asked.

"I've got a missile platform," Kris said.

"Take it out with lasers."

"Will do."

"Do we have any more of those on scans?" I asked.

"Not yet, but these platforms came out from behind Phobos. I'm sending a message to the fleet to inform them about the missiles and platforms," Kris said.

"Good job. Keep it up," I said. I wished I could speak to the Zarc ambassador again. The UME seemed to have gathered quite a lot of Phobian technology.

"This is Shey."

"Report," I said.

"The Monarchs can't activate their phasing drive while in atmo, so we ripped apart most of them, but two managed to get through. Requesting new orders."

"I want you to fly to the opposite side of Phobos. I think the UME is hiding some surprises back there. Go find out what they've got."

"Wilco. Heading for Phobos. Good luck, sir."

"Thanks, and same to you."

"Aviators make their own luck, sir."

Before I could reply, the *Starwarden* took five hits from ionized missiles.

"Report!" I called out as soon as the ship's intercom was up again.

"Sir, this is engineering," Duval said. "We've lost two inertial dampers. Shields are down for good, sir. Another hit would cripple us."

"CIC, I need coordinates!" I said.

"Sending them to Richard now," Kris said.

"Fire a torpedo at them Richard."

"Firing!"

"Okay, Jade, let's get out of here," I said. "We're going to need to pull back until we can make some repairs."

"Understood, pulling back."

"How's the rest of the fight going?" I asked, contacting the Sky Marshal.

"We're winning," he said, "but with heavy losses. The skies of Mars will be ours soon."

I glanced over at the main holodisplay and saw that we were slowly beginning to outnumber the UME. Just then, five Passerine Battlebringers dropped out of a wormhole with the *Zochtil* behind them.

"Reinforcements are here," Admiral Slumnar announced.

"'Bout time the cavalry got here," Jade said.

I watched as the Battlebringers descended on the remaining Monarchs and shot continuous streams of antimatter at them. The Monarchs couldn't phase out for more than a few seconds, and, eventually, each of them ran into a beam of antimatter.

"This is Shey," my CAG called out. "I can't find anything here, sir."

"Okay, come on back. You guys are on mop up. Make sure all those ships are actually dead. I can't send out SAR shuttles until I know they won't be blown out of the sky."

"Will do, Captain."

I still thought that something wasn't right with Phobos, but if Shey hadn't picked anything up, there wasn't much I could do. I wasn't going to drop my guard, even if I didn't have much of a guard left to drop.

Captain, this is Bronski.

Bronski, I said. It*'s good to hear from you again. What's your twenty?*

We just entered the alien weapon facility.

It's an ion cannon, I informed him.

Okay, then we're in the ion cannon, sir. I think it's about ready to discharge again.

Disable it quickly, I said.

I didn't have time to relay an order to the helmsman to move the ship, so I flipped the override switch on my command chair. I quickly jerked the ship up fifty degrees and boosted to half-light. I was hoping to evade the ion bolt if it was headed toward my ship. With two inertial dampers down I felt the ship jump up, and I was pushed against my seat as we sped up to half-light.

"Slow us down and bring us back to our original heading," I told the helmsman, flipping off the override. "CIC, where did that ion blast go?"

"It hit the *Sky*, sir."

I swore. "Shey," I called out to my CAG again, "I have a change in mission for you. I need you to land on the *Sky*. They've lost all power, so you'll have to go in on your own."

"Sir," Shey said. "You want me to land without mass drivers?"

"Yes, I need communication with the *Sky*, and we have to evacuate the Sky Marshal. Also, send an escort back to the *Starwarden* to accompany my two SAR shuttles to the *Sky*."

"Aye, aye, sir. If this works I'd better get a medal."

"You will. Just do your job."

"Wilco."

Chapter 15
The Price of War

"Shey, are you in position yet?" I asked her, as she lined her ship up with the lifeless mass driver of the SFS *Sky*.

"Yes, sir. I'm going in."

"Could you move a little faster?" I asked.

"No, sir. I'm already doing a reckless sixty klicks."

I switched my personal holodisplay to the view from Shey's camera. I watched as she slowly entered the mass driver tube trying to stay perfectly aligned so as not to damage her ship.

"Watch out, Shey," I said, flinching as she nearly hit her wing against the wall.

"Who's the aviator here?" she asked.

"Sorry," I said. "Just do your stuff."

I watched her get nearer. "I'm almost there," Shey said. "I'm running on maneuvering thrusters, and they aren't built for this kind of precision work. I'm supposed to have thousands of klicks of space to fly in, not four meters of mass driver tube."

"You've only got another hundred meters. Okay, okay. You've only got fifty meters."

"Ten KPH," Shey responded.

"Just bring her in nice and careful."

"I've got no choice but to bring her in slow," Shey shot back at me.

"Twenty meters," I said.

"Five KPH," Shey replied. "Deploying landing gear … Touch down! And do you expect me to fly out of this thing without a mass driver, too?"

"Yes," I said. "I need you to get back to your space wing as soon as you can. The mass driver might not be up and running for another couple of days."

"Great."

I watched as about fifty dockhands swarmed the ship. She handed out all the comm gear she had: her watch, her in-ship communicator, her emergency life pod communicator, even her ship's camera. The only thing left was her implant. Once she'd handed over her camera, I had to watch everything from her implant. She also gave them her flashlight, laser rifle, and emergency tool kit.

I'm ready to roll, she said.

Then get out of there.

Will do.

I watched Shey warm up her spacecraft and prepare for take off.

If I survive this, Shey said. *You owe me a drink.*

A drink and maybe even a day of liberty, I said.

She revved up her engines and took off. She blasted straight out of the mass driver. She obviously wasn't going too slowly, but she didn't have a choice. Just as she was exiting the tube, her ship hull hit the bottom of the tube, and I could feel her ship shudder as she scraped off some of the paint.

Shey, you okay? I asked.

You're paying for this, Skipper. And, sir?

Yes.

Never ask me to do that again, sir.

"If anything shoots the *Sky*, it's dead," I said, focusing my attention back on the bridge, now that Shey was safely out of the *Sky*. "The Sky Marshal is still on that ship. We need to shield him."

"We could create a sphere of ships and make any ship run the gauntlet to reach the *Sky*," Ardent suggested.

"I like that idea," I said. "Bronski, report!"

"We've got the ion cannon locked down, sir. Waiting for back-up."

"General Cestari should be there with the troop carriers shortly," I informed him. "Just hold tight." I switched comm channels. "*Caledonia*, this is *Starwarden*.

"*Starwarden, Caledonia*, this is McCloud."

"McCloud, I need the *Caledonia* to move to the coordinates I'm sending you. The *Sky* is disabled, and I need your help in providing cover for the *Sky*."

"Understood, I'll be there."

"Lauren," I said, switching channels again.

"Lauren here."

"Lauren, I need you to stage the remaining grapeshot frigates near the *Sky* and help the *Caledonia* and the *Starwarden* form a shield around her."

"Okay," Lauren said, "my ships are moving. Good luck."

"Thanks."

"Almek. Come in, Almek. This is Sky Marshal Kitt."

"It's great to hear your voice Sky Marshal," I said with relief.

"You have no idea how great it is to be holding a working piece of technology. I have sailors floating around my ship to pass messages back and forth. We're slowly opening bulkheads manually. And we're a giant sitting duck just waiting for any UME poachers."

I explained Ardent's shield idea and how the available ships were being deployed.

"We're doing everything we can to protect you," I said in conclusion.

"How's Bronski doing on the surface?"

"He has control of the ion cannon," I said.

"What are your evac plans?"

"Well," I said. "The *Caledonia* and I have a total of four SAR shuttles. As soon as we have the shield in place, I'll be sending them out to pick up your crew. You'll be the first off the ship."

"No," the Sky Marshal said. "This is my ship. If you've got the shield set up, I'll worry about getting my ship operational."

"Sir, you don't have a working holodisplay. Your job is to run the war. You can command the marines much better from my bridge than from the *Sky*."

"Bring a holodisplay over. I'll leave as soon as the marines arrive, but I want to help get my ship back together."

"Sir, that's the *Sky* captain's and the engineers' job, not yours."

"Almek, quit arguing and get moving."

"Yes, sir. I'll have my shuttles out in five."

"Okay," the Sky Marshal said. "We'll be ready."

***

"Sir, the troop transports have arrived," Jade informed me.

"Finally," I said. "We've already made ten round trips. How long before a SAR can pick up the Sky Marshal?"

"Two minutes."

"Sky Marshal, this is Almek."

"I see 'em, Almek," he replied. "I'm headed down to the airlock now."

"Okay, good. How is the *Sky* doing?"

"We're getting things back together. The ion cannon did some serious mischief to the matter-antimatter reactor. I don't understand it all, but the Passerines think they can get the reactor back online in a few more hours. From there, the rest of the ship's systems should start clicking into place."

"Good. You'll have to hustle down to the airlock now. The SAR will be there in a minute and twenty."

"This is Commodore Hunter. We're escorting the transports that just arrived. Sir, look at Phobos."

I glanced over at the holodisplay in the center of the bridge and swore. I watched at least a hundred tornadoes coming from the surface of Phobos and heading toward the transports.

"Where were they hiding?" I demanded of CIC.

"I'm not sure, sir."

"We need to reform the shield around the *Sky*," I said.

"Sir, this is Kris. We can't maintain a spherical shield against that many ships. The only chance the *Sky* has is for us to break formation and quickly engage targets of opportunity."

"What if she gets hit from Mars while we're engaging Phobos?" I asked.

"Sir," Kris said, "the *Sky* will be destroyed if we do nothing."

"Fine," I said in exasperation, "all ships break formation and attack the tornadoes. Protect the *Sky* at all costs."

"Shey," I began.

"I'm already engaging the tornadoes, sir."

"Good, thank you." I quickly switched to the SAR. "How long?"

"I've docked, and the Sky Marshal is aboard. Undocking in ten seconds."

"Sir, this is CIC. We're detecting a major power surge from the surface!"

I watched as multiple laser bolts shot up from the surface and riddled the *Sky*. One of them obviously hit the core, because the *Sky* blew up in a cloud of debris.

"SAR One!" I called out.

"Sir, I believe we are clear of the debris," the coxswain mate responded. "The Sky Marshal is aboard."

Then I watched in horror as a tornado emerged from the debris cloud and fired two missiles right up the six of the SAR. It went up in a fireball.

"SAR One, do you read? Sky Marshal Kitt! Coxswain mate first class Rand, do you read? SAR One, do you read?"

"Sir," Kris said. "SAR One is destroyed. All hands are lost."

"No," I said to myself. "CIC, tag that fighter! Shey, do you see the fighter I just tagged?"

"Yes, sir."

"Break off! Search and destroy!"

"Sir?" Shey asked.

"That's the fighter that killed the Sky Marshal!"

"Roger that, sir!" Shey said. "I'll blow that bastard out of the sky!"

I sat in silence for a moment until I saw Shey destroy the fighter. I watched as the remaining tornadoes were taken out.

"We've destroyed all remaining fighters," Shey reported.

"Good job. Form up with the transports again."

"Yes, sir."

"Emily," I said. "Connect me with the Sky Marshal."

"Sir?" Emily asked. She looked at me as if I'd finally gone mad.

"Connect me with Sky Marshal Michaela Cestari," I repeated.

"Oh, right, sir. Aye, aye, sir."

"General Cestari," I said.

"This is Cestari."

"Did you see what just happened?" I asked.

"Yeah. Is the Sky Marshal okay?" she asked.

"Yeah," I said. "As long as you're good, then I'd say the Sky Marshal is okay."

"I'm fine, but what does that have to do with the Sky Marshal?" I counted to three. "Are you saying…" she trailed off, not wanting to finish the thought.

"That is correct, Sky Marshal Cestari. Sky Marshal Kitt was killed in action. You are now in command."

"I see," Cestari said. It almost looked as if a physical weight had dropped on her shoulders. "We'll be in atmo in five."

Part 3
The End of the War

Chapter 16
Tunnels of Mars

"We're landing now," Sky Marshal Cestari said.

"Are you ready for this?" I asked. I was partially referring to taking Mars while also referring to her being the new Sky Marshal.

"I'm not sure," the Sky Marshal said. "It will take some adjustment not to have Sky Marshal Kitt available for help and support."

"I've still got the Sky Marshal's voice in my ear," I said, in an attempt to lighten her mood.

"Shut up, Almek," she said.

"Sorry," I said. "I'll give you all the intel you need, and I'll help you in any way I can. It looks like your force stayed pretty well intact when they came down through the atmo. I need some of your men to relieve Bronski's team at the ion cannon. Bronski needs to get his joint spec ops team down the rabbit hole, so they can find the Phobian ship."

"I know, Almek. One of my shuttles was delayed," the Sky Marshal said. "They were hit by debris while entering atmo, and their computer was damaged, but they're back on track now. They'll be there shortly."

"Good," I said. "Because every second we waste gives a new opportunity to the UME. Give me a second, I'm switching to Bronski."

"Understood."

"Bronski," I said. "Are your teams ready?"

"Yes, sir. I've got eyes on the shuttle."

"Okay, sit tight," I said. "The shuttle will be down shortly."

"Sir," Bronski said, "with all due respect, the shuttle will be here in a matter of minutes. We need to move now. Thomas hacked into the computers here. We were able to identity the location of the

Phobian ship. I want to leave now, sir."

"Okay, go for it," I said. "Sky Marshal?"

"Yeah," she said, "what is it, Almek?"

"I just talked with Bronski," I said. "He's anxious to head out, so I gave him the go ahead. Let your men in the shuttle know that the ion cannon is empty."

"You should have consulted me first, Almek. That isn't a decision you were authorized to make."

"Sorry, again," I said. "But, ma'am, they're currently under my command. Do I not have authority to make such a decision?"

"Yes, but it's against SOP to desert an enemy weapons fortification."

"Understood, ma'am. I need to adjust to your leadership style."

"Fine," the Sky Marshal said after a momentary pause. "Do things the way you always would during this battle. After that, we need to sit down and a talk. I'm the new Sky Marshal, and I'm not Bartholomew Kitt."

"Aye, aye, ma'am," I said.

"We'll discuss this later, I have a battle to command. I want an update on Bronski."

"Understood. Bronski what's happening?"

"We're already in the tunnels, sir," Bronski said, "and I'm pretty sure these weren't made recently."

"If you'll allow me," one of the Passerines joined our conversation. "I've run some preliminary tests on a sample I pulled out of the wall. These tunnels were made thousands of years ago. I'd bet on these tunnels being Phobian."

I turned to face Emily. "Emily, I want you to patch the Sky Marshal into my conversation." I figured this was something the Sky Marshal needed to hear.

"Will do, sir...she's patched in now, sir."

"So much for the Zarc assurance that the Phobians had never been on Mars," I said. "It appears that the Phobians had a rather large base here."

"Immense, sir," the Passerine continued. "I'd bet these tunnels span all of Mars."

"Say again," I requested. "I don't think I heard you right."

"It is my professional opinion," the Passerine repeated, "that this system of underground tunnels spans the whole equator of Mars and branches out to many other locations off the equator."

"Are you saying that this may have been their main base?" I asked.

"Yes, sir. I believe they originated from Phobos, but it looks to me like they moved here in massive numbers. They apparently were able to completely fool the Zarc. None of the tech here looks damaged. It doesn't look like there was ever a battle here."

"Do you think there are any of them still here?" the Sky Marshal asked, speaking up for the first time and echoing a fear that I had begun to harbor.

"I cannot make a determination on that," the Passerine replied. "Anything I said would be pure speculation, so I won't even try to guess."

"Very well. Carry on."

"Have you encountered any sentries yet?" I asked Bronski.

"No, not yet. Either they didn't think we would be able to reach their tunnels, or they're just too busy planning something big to worry about a couple people penetrating their tunnels. Honestly, though, I think they expected to do much better in orbit. They don't seem to be prepared for a ground invasion. They definitely weren't prepared for multiple species working together to defeat them."

"Yeah," I said, "but if the UME can get that Phobian ship airborne, the loss of their own ships won't have mattered a bit."

"Yes, sir," Bronski said. "That's why we have to make sure they don't ever get that baby off the ground."

I turned on my holodisplay and switched it from the display of the fleet in orbit to the display from Bronski's implant. I watched them work their way through the maze of tunnels, and I began to realize one of the reasons they may not have run into any sentries yet. There were just too many tunnels to have them all guarded.

"Bronski," I said, "they're going to have their guards at the entrance to the Phobian ship's hangar."

"I agree," Bronski said. "We'll be coming up on that tunnel shortly."

"I'm picking up heat signatures ahead of us," Scourge said, from his position in the lead.

"I've got them, too," Bronski agreed. "Four of them. Scourge, you and me, we'll take 'em out."

"Roger that," Scourge said.

They positioned themselves around the corner from the heat signature, and then they both rolled into the tunnel and came up on one knee firing into the enemy. Each of the four guards went down with a bullet to the brain.

"Clear," Scourge said after the last guard fell. The rest of Bronski's team came around the corner, and they advanced to a ledge that looked out into the hangar.

"Wow," was all Bronski managed to say. I heard one of the Passerines behind him whisper the name of their god. Personally, I was speechless.

They stood on a ledge that was about ten klicks above the base of the hangar, but the ship towered high above the ledge. It looked like it went up for at least another klick. I had known the Phobian ship would be large, but this was ridiculous.

"Sir," Thomas spoke up. "I'm registering some really strange readings coming from the ship. I think it's about to launch."

Bronski looked up, and I was able to see the giant hangar doors slowly start to open.

"Sky Marshal!" I shouted out loud *and* in my implant. I noticed multiple people glance over at me on the bridge, but I ignored them.

"What is it?" she said in a calm voice.

"The Phobian ship is preparing to launch!"

"Get your men inside it and prevent the launch. Prepare everyone in orbit for emergency evac. We can't defeat that ship if it makes it into orbit. Keep me informed."

"Will do," I said. I passed the orders to Commander Dale, so she could relay the orders to the fleet. I then turned my attention to Bronski and his men. I watched as the Passerines each picked up a human and flew them over to the ship.

"Wish us luck!" Bronski said, as he and the wingman commander landed on the hull of the Phobian ship.

"Good luck," I whispered.

"Breach the hull," Bronski ordered.

I watched as Scourge and Ed tried to use a laser torch to cut through the armor plating of the ship.

"That's not working," the wingman commander said.

"Try explosives," Bronski said.

Scourge placed small explosive charges on the ship and they all backed off. Four explosions later and there were four black scorch marks on the hull.

"Find an airlock," I ordered. I didn't like micromanaging my men, but we were running very short on time.

"Yes, sir," Bronski said.

They split up and started searching the hull.

"I've got something!" a Passerine shouted.

"What?" Bronski asked rushing over. "Yup, it's an airlock. Ed, hack into it."

"Like that'll be easy," Ed muttered under his breath.

I couldn't do anything but watch as Bronski paced and Ed struggled to break through the security system of an advanced alien race. Bronski switched his vision to infrared, but wasn't able to detect any temperature variation along the armor of the ship.

"This thing has amazing armor," Bronski commented

"I'm in!" Ed shouted five long minutes later.

The airlock opened, and they all piled in. The ship was more alien than the *Zochtil* or the *Cloudstep*. I had a hard time recognizing anything inside. Everything was odd. Bronski quickly searched the file the Cabal had given us and found directions to what we thought was most likely the bridge.

"Let's go!" he said.

Three klicks later and without any resistance, they made it to the bridge. There they found fifty UME naval personnel working frantically over alien controls and human keyboards.

"Wow," Bronski gasped.

"Don't kill anyone!" I shouted. I was momentarily drawn out of Bronski's world when Jessica responded to me.

"What, sir?"

"Not you," I said, glancing around my own bridge.

I turned back to Bronski's view.

Don't kill any of them. We need to know how to run the ship.

How do you want us to play this one out?

Your call. I'm sure you can figure it out.

"OKAY!" Scourge shouted. "EVERYONE, HANDS IN THE AIR!"

The looks on the sailors' faces were priceless as they turned to see Scourge leveling his SCAR at them.

"Kill them," the captain of the ship said.

The STARs and Wingmen stiffened but none of the sailors moved. Then two small orbs popped out of the floor and floated in front of the spec ops teams.

"RUN!" Bronski and I shouted at the same time.

Every one of the spec ops soldiers ran except for Scourge who flipped his SCAR to EMP mode and fired quick bursts at the orbs. Both clattered to the floor.

"I SAID PUT YOUR HANDS UP!" he shouted again.

"Sir," a watchstander said to the captain. "I'm detecting a comm link."

"Kill it."

"Damn it!" I swore, punching my chair, as the implant feed died, and I returned to my world on the bridge. "Commander Dale, give me a run down on our situation. I've got the deck."

Chapter 17
The Phobian Warship

"Sir," a watchstander shouted, "I've got the Phobian ship on my screens! They've left the hangar!"

I took a deep breath. I didn't have a clue what Bronski was up to, so I had to assume he was dead.

"This is Captain Manning, all ships prepare to engage the Phobian warship. We don't know what will work against them so prepare to fire everything at once. Sky Marshal Cestari has things under control on the surface. We must defeat the UME! This ship is all that stands between us and defeat of the UME."

"Torpedoes are loaded, nuclear, anti-matter, and standard," CIC reported. "All laser banks are ready. And Passerine antimatter beams are standing by."

"Understood, CIC."

"The ship has left atmosphere."

"All ships form up with the *Starwarden*. Grapeshot frigates ready for a run?" I shivered, knowing that Lauren was among them.

"We're ready," Lauren said.

"On my mark."

"I'm detecting a lot of energy building up on the ship," Jessica said.

"Mark!" I said, hoping that I hadn't issued Lauren's death sentence.

The grapeshot frigates shot ahead of the larger ships, achieving 0.2 of c in a matter of seconds. As they hurled grapeshot at the Phobian warship, it shot out a few short bursts at the grapeshot frigates. Half of them were destroyed instantly, without any trace they had ever existed.

"CIC, did that do anything to the Phobian ship?" I asked.

"No, sir."

"Grapeshots keep running," I ordered. "You didn't touch the ship."

"Wilco," Lauren said, her voice shaking.

"Get us close enough to use our antimatter beams. All other ships stay back. Emily, I want a direct line with the Passerines on our antimatter beams."

"This is Culmak," a Passerine said.

"Culmak, I'm not sure how to beat this thing, but we're going to try the antimatter beams. I've got Jade at the helm, and she'll pilot us over the ship."

"Understood. I'll keep you up-to-date."

"Thanks," I said. "Jade, you ready for this?"

"Yes, sir."

"Okay, fly us as close as possible and watch out for novel weapons."

"Thanks for the brilliant advice, Captain."

"Let's go!" I ordered. "Emily, get DC on the line."

"This is Damage Control."

"I want DC teams one through five with the Kelven drive and six through eight with the antimatter beams. And spread the other seven teams throughout the ship."

"Will do, sir."

"We're in beam range," Culmak said.

"Commence firing!" I ordered.

"No one has fired back yet, sir," Jessica said.

"Bridge, CIC," Kris said. "We're being targeted by the same weapons that took out the Grapeshots."

"Understood," I said. "Jade, can you jink to try and disrupt their firing systems?"

"Captain," Jade said, her voice tense. "I'm piloting a battleship, the flagship of the Alliance. You want me to *JINK*!"

"Good point," I said. "Well at least don't fly straight."

"Sir," Kris' voice came over the comm. "We've been hit by at least fifteen of the beams that annihilated the Grapheshots."

"Say again," I requested, not understanding.

"I don't understand it either," Kris said after repeating her statement, "but the weapons had no effect on us. We're still firing on the enemy ship."

"Any damage?"

"Sir," Culmak said. "We've been able to penetrate the first three feet of armor plating with the beams."

"Three feet!" I exclaimed. "Jade, reverse course. Let's see if Culmak can punch all the way through."

"Wilco."

"Sir," Kris said. "I've got a large orb in front of us. It appears to be charging weapons."

"Transfer the image to my holo."

I saw an orb that looked like a larger version of the thing that attacked the STARs aboard the Phobian vessel.

"Use the EMP grapeshot now!" I ordered.

Kris passed the order down, but not fast enough. Before the grapeshot could take out the orb, the orb destroyed one of our antimatter beams. "We lost an antimatter beam."

"Culmak?" I called out.

"I'm here, sir. But we suffered heavy casualties."

"Acknowledged, keep firing," I instructed and them immediately switched my circuit to medical. "Medical, dispatch a triage team to the antimatter beams."

"We've got more orbs in front of us," Kris said. "Targeting!"

I heard a voice in the background of CIC.

"Make that behind us, too," Kris said. "And we don't have a grapeshot array on our stern, sir."

"Jade, can you turn us around?" I asked.

"Yes, sir. Now?"

"Not yet. Kris, how long till the ones ahead of us are destroyed?"

"Thirty seconds."

"Turn around in twenty-five seconds."

"Will do, sir."

"Sir!" Kris shouted. "The orbs behind us have just destroyed our sub-light thrusters!"

I swore. "Jade, do we have any maneuverability?"

"Almost none, sir."

"Can you kick us up to k-speeds?"

"No, sir."

I swore. "Damage control?"

"I've got teams headed down there, but I only had one team stationed at the engines."

I cussed myself out. I shouldn't have micromanaged my DC teams. "Sorry. My fault," I said.

"You're the captain, sir."

"Just get them repaired ASAP."

"Understood. I'll give you an update in five."

"If we're still alive," I said to myself. "CIC, use lasers, missiles, anything against those orbs."

"Sir," Kris said. "They've stopped firing."

"What?" I asked.

"I don't know why, sir. But the enemy appears to have stopped firing."

"You have a transmission inbound," Emily said.

"Who from?" I asked

"The Phobian vessel, sir."

"Patch it in."

"Captain Almek Manning, this is the Phobian Warship. Come in Almek Manning."

"This is Almek Manning."

"Almek! It's good to hear your voice. This is Captain Bronski! We have temporary control of the ship, but I'm not sure for how long."

"Can you give me some details, Bronski?"

"Not really, sir. Thomas has tapped into the ship's systems and temporarily has control of them. But I can't guarantee anything unless we capture the bridge. I really need some back up to have a sporting chance."

"I'll try to get some marines there, but no promises."

"Thanks. I'll try to hold the fort."

"Sky Marshal," I called out. "Bronski needs marine back up on the Phobian warship."

"Understood," the Sky Marshal said. "I need everyone down here, though."

"With all due respect, if the UME keep this ship, we've lost the entire op. It wiped out half of my grapeshot frigates with one shot, and the *Starwarden's* thrusters were destroyed right after that."

Cestari swore. "I'll send up a hundred marines, but that's all I can spare. Tell Bronski he'll have back up in thirty."

"That's not fast enough, sir," Bronski said. "We need back up now."

"Bronski, I'm out of options. You and the other spec ops teams are the only soldiers I have."

"Sir," Drumair said. "All Passerine sailors are trained for boarding action. We can send over a couple hundred Passerines."

"Okay, Drumair, gather your teams fast and lead them over. Bronski you'll have a couple hundred Passerines over there in ten."

"Thanks. We should be able to hold off the UME for that long."

"Captain," the DC officer said, "we've got the engines at five percent. It'll be another half hour before we get to ten, and that is the best we'll be able to do. We're going to need a dry dock."

"Understood. Give me as much as you can." I turned back to Jade. "Can you slow us down now?"

"I'm turning us around right now, sir."

***

"Sirs," Richard said, facing the usual group, "this was not a warship."

"You said as much in your report," Sky Marshal Cestari responded, "but what type of ship was it? That's what we're all here to find out?"

"Yes, ma'am," Richard acknowledged. "The ship was designed as a colony ship."

"It's awfully big for a colony ship," Jack said.

"It wasn't just any old colony ship," Richard replied. "It was an intergalactic colony ship."

That sentence hung in the air for a long while before anyone spoke up.

"You mean it has a drive capable of covering intergalactic distances?" Jack asked.

"Yes," Richard stated.

"Do you have any data on the drive?" I asked. "Can you reverse engineer it?"

"Maybe," Richard said. "I've already got people at The Lab working on it, but I don't have enough people to go through everything we've uncovered."

"Okay," the Sky Marshal said. "So, what can we do with this ship?"

"Study it," Richard said. "Thomas was able to create a clever workaround which gives us control of most of the ship... more than the UME had access to. However, this isn't a warship, and we shouldn't try to use it as such."

"Okay," a Marine General said. "Then can we send it out to seek help from another galaxy?"

"We would just as likely find more enemies," Jack said with a wry smile.

"And based on my brief research," Richard added, "this drive will still take a year to get us to the nearest galaxy. I'd like to move this ship closer to The Lab. It would make it easier to study."

"Absolutely not!" the Sky Marshal said. "What if the ship has a self-destruct sequence that we accidentally trigger? No, I want this ship as far away from any of our colonies as possible."

"We could move it to Branson," Jack suggested. "The Lab has a large space facility in the Branson system that is in an opposite orbit as Branson itself."

"I love it," Richard said.

"Yes, that sounds good," the Sky Marshal agreed.

"I also have the spec ops teams still helping search the tunnel system under Mars. They haven't come up with anything major yet, but I'll keep you informed."

"Thank you," the Sky Marshal said, as Richard took his seat. "General Mack, can you give us an update on earth?"

"Well," the marine general said. "Mars was easy to take. The UME only allowed military personnel on the planet, so we didn't have to worry about collateral damage. On earth, that is far from the case. Also, the UME governments seem to have forgotten that they don't allow civilians to carry any lethal weapons, because my men have encountered civilians armed with mil grade assault rifles. It'll be a while before the UME stations on earth fall, but they *will* fall eventually."

"Ma'am," Richard said, standing up again. "You have to see this."

"Okay, let's see it."

The holoprojector was filled with the view from an implant of one of the soldiers on Mars. In the foreground was Lieutenant McFarland, and in the background was a massive tunnel with lightning sparking all around it.

"*What* is that?" Jack asked, leaning forward in his chair to get a better view.

"That is the question we're all asking, sir," McFarland replied. "I can tell you this much, my scanners indicate this tunnel exits out the back side of the planet and extends into space."

"That doesn't make any sense," I said. "Why haven't we noticed that before? If it extends into space, someone should have detected it."

"It appears to be cloaked once it exits the tunnel," McFarland said, "It's a needle-in-the-haystack proposition. This structure just gets smaller as it goes up. My guess is that it's barely a foot in diameter when it reaches space."

"So what is it?" Jack asked again, this time looking at Richard.

"I need more data, sir." His eyes had a faraway look. "Give me a second."

The holoprojector image switched over to Bronski.

"We're near the pole, about eighty degrees north of McFarland's equatorial position. I'm seeing the exact same field generator behind me."

Sure enough, there was an identical tunnel behind Bronski.

"Excuse me," I heard Ed say. "Scourge, come over here."

Scourge turned to face Ed instead of Bronski, and we saw Ed bending over an alien console.

"I've hacked into the first layer of code, and I've gained access to over a thousand yottabytes of data. Normally, we only carry a hundred yottabyte memory orbs on ops, but, for this one, I was carrying five hundred. But, there are still thousands of yottabytes more once I can crack through the protection."

"Can you set up a transmitter, or do you need me to get additional orbs for you?" Richard asked.

"I'll try and rig this thing–whatever it is–as a transmitter, so have The Lab ready to record as much data as I can transmit."

"I'll set it up," Richard said, killing the projector. "If you'll excuse me, I'm needed elsewhere."

"Dismissed," Jack and Cestari said at the same time.

Chapter 18
Zarc Interference

"Captain Manning," I heard Emily say over the circuit in my stateroom.

"Yes, Emily."

"The Sky Marshal requests your presence at the conference room on Dalton Spaceways. However, she wants the *Starwarden* to stay here."

"Why didn't she call me herself?"

In spite of my question being rhetorical, Emily answered me. "She didn't call me, sir. I received word of the meeting through her assistant."

Something odd was up.

"Emily, tell Shey to warm up her spacecraft. She's taking me to Dalton Spaceways at max speed. I need to be there about fifteen minutes ago."

"I'll let her know."

By the time I reached the hangar, I found Shey already in her ship and waiting for me.

"What's up?" she asked, as I slid into the seat behind her.

"I'm not sure, but whatever it is, something big is going down. So, get us there quickly, and we'll both find out."

"Wilco. Commodore Hunter requesting permission to launch."

"Permission granted. Good luck, you two," Jade said.

"Brace yourself," Shey warned me.

I was pushed back in my seat with about seven g's of force. The *Starwarden* was still orbiting Mars so that we could remain right next to the Phobian ship, which wasn't scheduled to fly to Branson for another week. Shey had me at Dalton Spaceways in twenty minutes. Completely ignoring the space traffic controller who told her to wait her turn to dock, Shey dove in front of an Academy SAP and landed smoothly in the hangar.

She locked her craft down and jumped out just a few seconds behind me.

"I'm coming with you."

"You'd better," I said, as I took off sprinting down the halls. "DSF MP's are going to want your hide after that stunt you pulled. Let's just hope Jack gets you off the hook."

"Tell me about it. I've done a lot of hot-dogging in my time as an aviator, but that was the craziest parking job I've ever done. DSF would be within their rights to bar me from returning."

I knew that things were going to be really bad as soon as I walked in. The first indicator was the small number of people around the table. The only ones present were the Sky Marshal, the High Admiral, Jack Dalton, Richard, and Bronski, of all people. The figure that really had me worried was the all-too-familiar purple cloud of the Zarc Ambassador.

"Sorry I'm late," I said.

"That's fine," the Sky Marshal replied. "Let's get this meeting officially kicked off. What did you wish to discuss Ambassador?"

"The Phobian vessel and the planet you've commandeered."

"We asked for your assistance, and you denied it," Jack said.

"I had to confer with my superiors. They have come to a decision."

"They're too late," Cestari said. "We already won that battle."

"That's not relevant to their decision."

"What is their decision?" the High Admiral asked.

"The Phobian vessel and the planet the Phobians occupied must be destroyed."

"WHAT!" Every person in the room shouted in unison.

"No way!" Bronski said. "We lost two wingmen and five other passerines when we captured that ship."

"Not to mention the blood the was spent to buy Mars. You can't just waltz in and take them away."

"Actually we can," the Zarc cloud said. "We are far more advanced than you are. You cannot resist us. However, we do not wish to kill any of you. We are in an alliance with you after all."

"It doesn't sound like much of an alliance," Jack muttered.

"I have orders to carry out, as do each of you."

"Actually, no one orders me around," Jack said.

"We do," the ambassador replied curtly. "All personnel will leave the vessel and the planet within one day. No Phobian objects shall be removed from either one. If anything is removed, it will be hunted down and destroyed without discrimination, collateral damage being expected in such circumstances. I'll return tomorrow."

And the Zarc cloud disappeared.

"That's no good," Richard said. "This was the breakthrough we needed. I *need* all this tech."

"Look, I don't care what the Zarc want…" the Sky Marshal started to say.

Shut up! Jack shouted over our implants. *I'm sure the Zarc have ears here. But I think our implants our secure.*

Agreed, the Sky Marshal said. As I was saying, *I don't care what the Zarc want. Let's scavenge as much as we possibly can.*

Do you really think we can succeed at smuggling some of this stuff off? I asked.

Maybe one or two small items could be removed without being noticed. Richard sounded really disappointed. *We're talking about a ship designed to travel between galaxies in less than a year, and we're going to lose that ship forever. Not to mention Mars. They want to destroy Mars!*

Did you ever figure out what the big generator on Mars was for? Jack asked.

I've got a couple ideas. I think it's a shield of some sort, but I'm not sure what it was for. Obviously, the UME never figured it out either.

This is going to take a while, the Sky Marshal said. *Captain Hunter, can you bring us dinner?*

Of course. I just have something I need to clear up with Mr. Dalton.

What is it, Shey?

I kinda pissed off space traffic control.

Jack laughed. *I'll let them know you were authorized to take all measures necessary to get here fast.*

Thank you, sir.

From Werf's, if you please, the Sky Marshal specified.

I'm on it.

***

"Captain Manning," Jade said

"What is it?" I asked. I was back on the bridge of the *Starwarden,* waiting for the Zarc to arrive.

"Over here, sir," Jade said.

I got up and walked over to a station where Jade was leaning over a petty officer.

"What am I looking at?" I asked.

"Petty officer," Jade said. "You show him."

"Well, sir," the petty officer began. "I was just running standard sensor readings. I'm scanning the debris in orbit."

"Okay," I acknowledged.

"Well," he continued. "I noticed something strange, so I zoomed in. Then I saw it. Right there. See?" He was pointing at a part of the display where nothing seemed to be happening.

"No, Petty Officer. I don't see anything."

His hands flew across the controls, and he replayed the last five seconds. He did it three more times.

"Petty Officer, I'm still not seeing anything. Just explain what you want me to see."

"Okay, how about now?" His hands flew across the keyboard again, and his display changed to different colors, mostly blue. But, in the sector he had been pointing at, I could see a short flash of green.

"I saw it that time. What is it?" I was beginning to lose patience.

"That was our extra-dimensional sensor display. It's still experimental, but it's supposed to help us see things that are traveling through a different dimension. It could be a UME ship or an alien ship. I can't really tell."

"You called me over here to tell me you don't know what you're seeing?"

"Sir, I double-checked. Then I had Lieutenant Robinson check and, I also called down to engineering and Commander Duval also checked. It's not a malfunction, and it's not one of our guys, so there's something out there. I just wanted to let you know."

"Sky Marshal Cestari," I said. "I've got a petty officer up here who was running some routine scans. He identified an extra-dimensional signal that has now disappeared. My crew has thoroughly checked it, and it wasn't a malfunction."

"Okay," she said. "So what are you trying to say?"

"We've got some alien tech in orbit or passing through. We're not sure which, but it appears to be cloaked."

"Okay," the Sky Marshal said again after a pause. "Have that petty officer stop any other tasks and keep a close watch for that signature. The moment you get more intel, contact me."

"Will do. Petty Officer, keep working this. I need you to find that signature again."

"Wilco, sir."

"Looks like a Zarc ship," Jade said, pointing at a different display.

Obviously the Zarc didn't trust us. We'd never encountered them cloaking before. Or perhaps we'd never noticed them cloaking before.

"Sky Marshal, Jack, are you guys seeing this?" I called out.

"Yeah," Jack responded. "I'm trying to contact them right now. Get to your stateroom, and I'll patch you in."

"Wilco," I said. "Petty Officer, run through all our scan logs. I want to know how long that ship has been here."

"Yes, sir."

A few minutes later, I was hooked into a circuit with the Zarc ambassador and his superior.

"Look," Jack said. "You guys are decades ahead of us."

"Hundreds of your years," the superior corrected.

Decades, Jack said again, but just to me. "Exactly. Surely, you have some way of shutting down all the Phobian tech on the planet without destroying the planet itself. It's a valuable military base. We're allies after all, aren't we?"

"The Phobian technology is dangerous. You're not advanced enough to deal with their technology. We must eliminate it."

"Sir," the petty officer said, "that ship has been in orbit above Mars since a month before the battle."

"Thanks."

Jack, I've got something to say. May I cut in here? I asked.

Go for it, Jack said, exasperated.

"I saw your ships watching us the day we took Mars," I said.

"That's impossible," the superior said.

I quickly pulled up the scanner records and read back his exact location. "You saw how much we paid to capture Mars. We lost one of our best military commanders, Sky Marshal Kitt. We're not going to give up that planet without a fight. Even if it means we lose more people."

"Are you threatening us?"

"I already know how to track your ship, and we currently have control of the Phobian warship. We're willing to give the warship to you in exchange for the planet. Otherwise, we'll use the warship to defend the planet."

The screen died.

I hope you didn't just screw this up, Jack said.

Believe me, I hope so, too.

We waited for ten minutes. Then the screen flared to life again.

"We have a polymer we can use to coat the tunnels and destroy any Phobian technology. However, this polymer is extremely dangerous and has a half-life of a thousand years. So, do not ever try to tunnel through Mars, or you will die. We do expect you to leave the Phobian warship within twenty minutes."

"It will be done," Jack said. *Thanks, Almek!*

***

"Richard," the Sky Marshal said.

It had been almost a week since the Zarc intervention.

"Well," Richard began, "I've got bad news. Very bad. I assume that most of you have watched the reports that were sent in from the joint spec ops group." Most of the people at the table were nodding their heads. "Well, the generator they discovered was a shield generator. I couldn't begin to guess where it got the power necessary to keep it going. The generator created a shield that reached all the way out to Pluto's orbit. It shielded the whole system."

"That's not possible," Admiral Andrus said.

"I've never heard of anything that powerful, even in the myths of the Phobians," Numair said.

"Even I find this hard to believe," Jack added.

"I can't explain it, but based on the data the spec ops teams gathered, it is the truth."

"What did it protect us from?" I asked.

"That's what I'm getting at," Richard said. "It prevented any Draconian or Garm from entering our system."

I swore in every language I knew, and I wasn't the only one.

"So the Zarc just destroyed our most powerful asset?" I asked.

"Yes," Richard said.

"That does explain why the Draconians only set up a blockade and didn't just bomb your world to ashes," Sonnel said. "I'd always wondered about that."

"I had wondered the same thing," Numair agreed.

"So, now the Draconians could invade our space at any time?" I asked, not really wanting to hear the answer.

"Yes," Richard said. "In fact, I expect the Draconians to be here within six months. After we destroyed their blockade, they have often sent out drones to survey our system. Of course we have destroyed them, but they will eventually learn that we are no longer protected."

We all sat in silence for a moment, contemplating that possibility.

"Do you have any good news?" Jack asked.

"Well," Richard said. "There isn't much. We were able to recover quite a lot of data about Phobian weapons. The Lab is working on creating prototypes. We've got a couple UME scientists working with us now, so it shouldn't be long before we've got some nice additions to our arsenal. The level of ion technology the Phobians have will help us make improvements over our EMP grapeshot by leaps and bounds."

Chapter 19
Dealing with O'Brien

Captain McFarland, commander of DSF's most deadly strike team, Blue Squadron, faced down Chairman O'Brien and a small contingent of red-clad Council Guard Marines.

"What is your problem?" O'Brien asked McFarland as he stepped in front of the Chairman.

"You are," McFarland said with a wry grin.

"And what is that supposed to mean?"

McFarland pulled out a set of handcuffs. "You are under arrest by order of Jack Dalton, owner of this station. Jack Dalton has filed a complaint against you, Dalton v. the esteemed Chairman O'Brien."

"Get your hands off me, young man!" O'Brien said. He tried and failed to break McFarland's iron grip. "Do you realize who I am? Maybe you are a little behind on the news. I was just elected to be Chairman of the Presidential Council and am now ruler of all humans."

"Actually, that's not true," McFarland said. "I am a human who is not under your authority."

"Guards!" O'Brien shouted at the marines, having given up reasoning with McFarland.

The marines had tensed up as soon as McFarland grabbed O'Brien, but there was the small matter of the other four members of Blue Squadron standing in front of them.

"What is he being charged with?" the captain of the Marine guard asked.

"Chairman O'Brien has been charged by Jack Dalton wit high treason against the Presidential Council and the Four Species Alliance. In addition, O'Brien is also charged with attempting to assassinate Captain Almek Manning and endangering the flagship of the Four Species Alliance by hiring Daniel Lee, a known traitor.

"Jack Dalton has painstakingly gathered evidence over the course of several years, and Mr. Dalton's agents have recently found files in UME databases that prove O'Brien's collusion with Daniel Lee and O'Brien's plans to kill the war hero, Almek Manning."

McFarland turned to face the Council Guard. "Do any of you wish to risk your life to prevent me from lawfully arresting this man?"

"Men!" O'Brien shouted. "This will be nothing but a kangaroo trial orchestrated by Jack Dalton and his goons. He must have gotten wind of the Council's plans."

"What plans?" McFarland asked, with obvious interest.

"I came here to discuss the Council's plan to absorb Dalton Space Force into the Solar Fleet to form a single, cohesive military force, but, after this, I'll strip everything from Jack. The Council will not tolerate this type of behavior."

McFarland smiled. "If any of you have evidence to produce, you will be exempted from any charges being filed against you if you come forward in the next forty-eight hours. An official notice will go out to all members of the Council Guard. I hope you make the right decision."

McFarland turned his back on the marines and pushed Chairman O'Brien toward a lift. None of the marines made a move to stop them.

I finally tore my eyes from the holodisplay and smiled at Jack Dalton. This was the justice I had hoped to see for a long time, and it was still quite welcome, even if I was seeing it a few hours after the fact.

"So it has finally happened?" I asked with a smile.

"It has," Jack said with an equally enthusiastic smile. "Like McFarland said, we've got the goods on him. We'll throw the book at him. And with the evidence we've gathered, he won't be able to wriggle out of it this time. He will finally be held accountable for his actions."

"Charles O'Brien has been a pain in my rear since I was aboard the *Mayflower* as a child. It will be a great day when he's no longer able to bother me."

"I knew you would feel that way. That's why I wanted you to see this. I considered letting you be there in person but decided it probably wasn't a good idea."

"Yeah, you're probably right on that count. So what was O'Brien talking about when he mentioned the Space Force?"

"Oh that," Jack said, chuckling to himself. "Apparently the Council wanted me to relinquish command of DSF and allow them to merge with the SF. Of course they had no legal basis to enforce their plan, so I told the Council any of my sailors could switch to the Solar Fleet if they wanted. O'Brien seems to think he'll survive the trial and afterward be able to steal all my property, but the Council isn't backing him up on that. In fact, when I shared my evidence with the council they decided not to put up a fight."

"He never was that popular among his fellow politicians. So when is his trial?"

"We're giving his inner circle two days to come clean. After that the trial starts. Captain Michelle Silver wasn't very happy about the short notice for her to prepare a case, but I wasn't very sympathetic."

"Oh yeah?" I asked. "What did you say?"

"I told her she should have started preparing for this case right after you were exonerated in your court-martial."

***

I was pleasantly surprised to find out that the prosecuting lawyer was my former girlfriend, Annabeth Gauge, who had escaped from London Proper with me. However, she asked that we not meet up until after the trial. I guessed that, even though it was a very solid case, she was still nervous about it because of the political stakes involved.

Two days later, I found myself sitting in the same courtroom where I had been tried for high treason several years earlier. It seemed fitting, and I was sure that Jack had taken care of scheduling that courtroom.

"All rise!" the bailiff ordered.

I smiled when I saw Judge Griffith walk into the courtroom.

"This is…," O'Brien began, before launching into a string of obscenities. "This is nothing but a show trial!"

"Chairman O'Brien," Judge Griffith said. "I suggest you restrain yourself. Captain Silver, please keep your client in line."

"Sir," Silver began. "I agree with the Chairman's sentiment. This is a show trial."

"Silver, I'll advise you to show proper respect for the bench if you want to avoid a finding of contempt against yourself."

"Sir," Annabeth said, standing up. I was surprised to see her wearing the dress blacks of Dalton Space Force. Apparently Jack was gathering more of my friends under his banner. "Can we begin?"

"Yes," Judge Griffith said. "I hereby call this court to order!"

Though Jack hadn't stacked the jury, everyone familiar with the facts of the case knew the outcome was inevitable. The trial featured two days full of evidence and witnesses that Jack Dalton had organized to leave O'Brien without any cover to hide behind.

I spent two of the most satisfying days of my life watching Charles O'Brien squirm as he heard each new piece of evidence and each new witness. Some of the witnesses were UME, some were part of his own guard, but each of them talked convincingly about the illegal acts O'Brien had committed.

At the close of the trial, Annabeth stood up and delivered an amazing closing statement.

"We have got quite a ground-breaking jury here. Because

Chairman O'Brien's crimes were committed against the Four Species Alliance, we have human, Canid, and Passerine jury members. Some of you are military, some of you are civilian. All of you have heard the evidence and the witnesses describing Chairman O'Brien's war crimes. This man betrayed the government which he represented, and the Alliance as a whole, by working with an enemy agent, by trying to kill one of the war heroes of the Alliance, Captain Almek Manning, and by trying to destroy the military asset that served as the keystone of the Alliance, namely, the *Starwarden*. The only documented motive for his actions is the undying hatred he bears against all of the surviving members of the good ship *Mayflower*. Based on the facts of the case, based on precedents in the legal systems of all four species, and based on O'Brien's callous disregard of the personnel and assets of the Four Species Alliance, I urge the death penalty as the only suitable punishment."

Captain Silver stood up. "Lieutenant Gauge tried to paint a picture of hatred borne by my client against Almek Manning. However, I must forcefully reiterate for the record that such hatred does not exist. On the other hand, Jack Dalton and Almek Manning do bear such hatred against Chairman O'Brien. O'Brien has served the global community well for many years and his skills are sorely needed to guide us through the present crisis. It is very clear that O'Brien's persecutors have arranged an entertaining show trail. Please do not play into their hands. Please act upon the plain facts of my client's record and declare him not guilty."

"Members of the jury, I believe the procedures we established for this court have been thoroughly explained to you. How long do you believe you will need to review the arguments that have been presented in this case?" the judge asked.

The foreman stood up. "I believe that all of us understand this system well enough, and I believe the facts have been very clear. I'd like to hold a public vote now."

"This trial has already been unusual in other respects. Please proceed," the judge said.

The foreman turned to face the other eleven members of the jury. "All in favor of declaring Chairman O'Brien guilty of all charges, raise a hand."

Eleven hands shot into the air.

"I believe we have our verdict," the foreman said, turning back to the judge. "We unanimously find Chairman O'Brien guilty of all charges."

"So be it," Judge Griffith said. "I hereby strip Charles O'Brien of his title of Chairman. Mr. O'Brien you have been found guilty of high treason and, as such, your sentence will be death. The sentence will be executed twenty-four hours hence. You will be kept under guard of Blue Squadron until the sentence of the court is carried out. This court is now adjourned!" Judge Griffith banged his gavel and left the courtroom.

I had killed hundreds, maybe even thousands, of people by ordering the launch of an anti-matter torpedo or by giving orders to my bombers. Though I may have been joyous about the outcome of the battle, I was never glad to have to kill anyone. However, I had never felt so relieved as I did when I heard the judge pronounce the sentence against O'Brien.

"Annabeth, good job," I said, shaking her hand.

"Thanks," Annabeth said. "This was definitely my highest stakes court case ever."

"You did well. After the sentence is carried out, we should meet up at the Spaceman's Asteroid."

"Will do," Annabeth said and flashed a broad smile.

***

Recognizing that the tide had turned against him, O'Brien decided to follow in the footsteps of many despots and put on a show of bravado for the history books. After O'Brien was killed, I felt safer than I had in a long time. Even with the newly increased threat from the Draconians bearing down on the Alliance, I felt safe for the first time since we escaped from London Proper.

Annabeth, Kai, Jenny, Richard, and Kris were all at the Spaceman's Asteroid with me celebrating the defeat of the man who had tried to kill us as soon as we escaped from London Proper. Even Marian, one of my London Proper squad mates who had joined the marines, was there. We celebrated with Jack Dalton and many others. Tom the barkeep had made everything half-price in honor of the great day. Even the Sky Marshal joined us.

"Hey, Mr. Dalton!" a voice shouted from the entrance to the bar.

We all turned to see a young female reporter rushing in.

"Mr. Dalton," she said again. "Can I interview you about the trial?"

"Of course, Alanna," Jack said, smiling.

"Good."

A camera orb hovered out of its cradle on her shoulder and positioned itself between her and us.

Chapter 20
Return Home – George McCloud

"Take us down, Lieutenant Johnstone," Colonel-Skipper George McCloud ordered his navigator.

"With pleasure, sir. Helm, take us to Danderhall," Lieutenant Johnstone ordered.

McCloud leaned back in his chair as he watched the *Caledonia* move smoothly from orbit into Earth atmosphere. He watched on his holodisplay as troop carriers continued to glide down to Russia, which was still putting up a strong fight. He saw a couple Condor-class bombers returning to orbit from England to refuel and reload. England and Russia were the only countries left in the UME, but they refused to give in. The battles against the UME had been very successful, but the few UME soldiers left were still fighting with fierce determination. The war had deteriorated into a brutal slog.

The *Caledonia* circled Edinburgh twice then settled over a pasture north of Drum Wood. McCloud was anxious to land. This was the culmination of what he had dreamed of and fought for, ever since joining the Cabal. McCloud was returning home.

"Are you ready, George?" Major Delgetty asked.

"I certainly am," McCloud said. "I've been waiting for a long time. I just can't believe this moment has finally arrived."

"Landing in ten, sir," Johnstone said.

"Good, take her down."

George knew the entire crew was anxious for this moment. Though only a small percent of the crew had actually been Cabal members, they had grown together, and many of them had adopted Celtic traditions as their own. Some of the Passerines had developed a passion specifically for Scottish history and culture.

McCloud felt the strong pull of Earth's gravity as the *Caledonia's* gravity field was taken off-line. McCloud had almost forgotten what standard Earth gravity felt like.

"We've landed, sir," Lieutenant Johnstone said.

"Okay, keep her safe," McCloud told Delgetty. "And be ready with the fireworks."

"Don't worry, I will."

George McCloud left the bridge and went to the debarkation hatch. Along the way, he was joined by every member of the Cabal aboard, other than Major Delgetty, who had to stay with the ship. There was also one Passerine who joined the group. He had learned to play the bagpipes and had asked to join the four Cabal members who also played the pipes.

"Ready, darling," Kathy McCloud said, as she reached out to take George's hand.

"Part of me can't believe this is happening, but the other part is desperately hoping this is real."

From the quarterdeck, McCloud's gaze was drawn in the direction they would march. In the northwest, encircled by mist, he saw the rugged form of Arthur's Seat, and he knew he was finally home.

The shepherd who had agreed to let us use his pasture was waiting a hundred meters from the ship, with about fifty people.

"Good morning, sir," George shouted down the ramp as his men formed up behind him.

"Good morrow," the shepherd replied. "I can't believe that I've lived to see this day finally arrive."

As soon as George stepped onto his native soil, the pipes began playing "Hail Caledonia!" Originally written in the early twentieth century, the words had been adapted to serve as the anthem of the Cabal and had rapidly gained popularity among the civilians in the Scottish Underground. All the Cabal members joined in singing the lyrics, and, pretty soon, the locals also joined in.

Hail Caledonia! Land of my childhood,

Home of my birth, so radiant and fair.
Though I have gazed on heaven and its beauties,
Nowhere in space with thee can compare.
Thou art majestic and regal in splendour,
Thou art the land of the highland and lea.
Thy lads and lassies love thee so tender:
Hail Caledonia! Forever be free!

Help the Irish take back their Em'rald Isle
Where the four-leaved shamrock grows,
Let the English claim the sullied old Thames,
And the faded Tudor rose,
But give me the land of the heather and the kilt,
The mountain and the river,
For the blood leaps in my veins
When I hear the bagpipe strains:
Scotland, free from bondage forever!

Hail Caledonia! Birthplace of heroes
Whose names are inscribed on the parchment of fame.
New heroes now follow their noble example
That others will rally and honour thy name.
Scotsmen, I give you a toast, make it your toast,
Fill up your cups to leave the UME.
Here's to free Scotland, her lads and her lassies.
Long live Caledonia! We shall make thee free!

Help the Irish take back their Em'rald Isle
Where the four-leaved shamrock grows,
Let the English claim the sullied old Thames,
And the faded Tudor rose,
But give me the land of the heather and the kilt,
The mountain and the river,

CALEDONIAN CABAL

For the blood leaps in my veins
When I hear the bagpipe strains:
Scotland, free from bondage forever!

Hail Caledonia! Thy name acts like magic
On each Scottish heart when serving in space.
On distant Mars when their day's work is over
Their thoughts to dear Scotland will instantly race.
Thy sons are respected and loved by all worlds,
A Scotsman is always so faithful and true.
And if in battle his standard's unfurled,
He'll give his life's blood, Caledonia, for you!

As they marched toward Edinburgh, they alternated singing the anthem of The Cabal with other songs popular among Scottish patriots. A massive crowd joined behind the contingent of Cabal members, and they all joined in the singing. By the time the group reached Parliament, there were a total of fifteen people playing bagpipes, and many other instruments had also joined the procession. George was filled with pride for his countrymen as he heard the refrain echoed, "Forever be free!"

George led the group down into Holyrood Park, where a large podium had been set up for him, with cameras ready to transmit this moment throughout the system. George climbed up the steps and rested his arms on the podium. He signaled the conductor, took a deep breath, and waited for the song to finish on the toast of the Cabal: *Long live Caledonia! We shall make thee free!*

"People of Scotland," McCloud began. "I am Colonel-Skipper George McCloud of the Four Species Alliance Ship *Caledonia* and a proud member of the Caledonian Cabal." As soon as he mentioned The Cabal, he was interrupted by jubilant applause. "I served in the Caledonian Cabal for many years working to achieve our freedom from the UME. And *we have*! We have won on Mars. We have won on Titan. The UME has been beaten, and all that remains is to win back England and Russia. They cannot hold back the combined might of the Four Species Alliance. And that is what we have now joined. We have once again become the *free* and *independent* nation of Scotland, with this great city of Edinburgh as our capital. We have finally overthrown the oppressor and can now stand on our own, independent of England. We are *Scotland*! We are *Caledonia*! And now we are *free*!" Once again, the audience burst into wild applause.

At that very moment, the *Caledonia,* having just reached her position above Edinburgh Castle, fired all of her torpedo tubes, launching hundreds of fireworks into the air. After all, independence can't be claimed without fireworks. It just wouldn't be right. With Arthur's Seat–the Edinburgh landmark named for the most famous Celtic warrior of all time–providing a fitting backdrop, McCloud kissed Kathy while the fireworks burst overhead. Things were finally as they should be, and McCloud was as happy as he could ever have imagined being.

Chapter 21
Promotions

"It is my honor," the new Chairman of the Presidential Council said, "to present to you the new Sky Marshal of the Solar Military."

Jack Dalton had cleared a large food court. All of the stalls had been packed up and the shops that lined the edges of the food court were temporarily closed. Rows and rows of chairs floated one on top of the other, so that Jack could pack in as many people as possible. He had the chairs floating in such a way that each person could theoretically see the speaker. However, that wasn't quite true of everyone. Fortunately, I had a good view, because I was sitting on the podium with some of the top brass.

"Thank you," Sky Marshal Michaela Cestari said. She was stunning in her full dress whites, with numerous medals adorning her chest, and the golden sunbursts on her collar sparkling in the light.

Personally, I felt a little uncomfortable in my dress whites. I almost wished they were the dress blacks of the Space Force. I remembered turning down a full commission in the Force, and I had sometimes wondered if I'd made the right choice. Not that it really mattered, except on occasions like this. I was a member of the Alliance more than I was of the Solar Fleet.

"There are only two circumstances that require the promotion of an admiral or general to Sky Marshal. Those are the declaration of war or the death of the previous Sky Marshal, neither of which are causes for celebration," Cestari said. "I come before you today because the first Sky Marshal of the Solar Military died almost two weeks ago. He left large shoes to fill. Sky Marshal Bartholomew Kitt was an amazing man. He seemed to always have plans larger than anyone knew. He seemed to always know just how to push someone into doing the necessary thing. Personally, I believe that he chose the wrong person to be his replacement, but I accepted his call in this matter hoping the situation would never arise and knowing the life of an admiral would be easier..."

The Sky Marshal continued for five minutes. It was a very touching speech, but I spent most of my time just staring at the small crystal casket that held the ashes of the once great man. Jack had set up a hologram of Sky Marshal Kitt in the casket, so that, even though all we actually had of his body was debris from the explosion, it appeared that the man was lying at rest in the casket. Finally, it was my turn to get up.

"If it weren't for Sky Marshal Kitt, I wouldn't be alive today. Sky Marshal Kitt stood up for me in a military tribunal when I was a nobody charged with treason, just a kid who was hoping to get into the Academy. He guided me through the Academy, always ensuring I was in the right place at the right time. Then he pushed me into Dalton Space Force, as the Solar Fleet Liaison with Defense Force Delta. It was there that I gained my first combat experience and was promoted through the ranks and named commander of the defense orbitals above Branson. From there he led me to my current ship the *Starwarden*.

"However," I continued. "I was never very fond of the Sky Marshal. He was my CO, nothing more. Some people may have thought of him as a fatherly figure, but he never filled that role for me. He was always pushing me as hard as he could. He did everything possible to challenge me. He sent me to Branson as the only Solar Fleet officer. He pushed me into the command of the first integrated human-alien ship. He put my girlfriend on the front line, in a grapeshot frigate. He stole my best officers, giving me in return, new personnel to teach and train. He gave me assignment after assignment that was as tough as nails. Sky Marshal Kitt pushed me into whatever I have accomplished. I only hope that one day I can be half the leader he was." I saluted the figure in the crystal casket, executed an about-face, and returned to my seat.

After many other talks, the time arrived to send off the casket. Sky Marshal Cestari, Admiral Andrus, Jack Dalton, High Admiral Numair, High Alpha Sonnel the Third, and I were honored to be the casket bearers. We marched through the halls of Dalton Spaceways until we reached the antimatter torpedo tube. We waited while Jack gave the orders for the tube to be extended and while Dalton Spaceways positioned itself toward the sun. Jack nodded to a spaceman holding a trumpet, and we placed the casket into a specially crafted torpedo case. Then we loaded the torpedo into the tube. As the spaceman played the last note of taps, I pressed the button that fired the casket of Sky Marshal Bartholomew Kitt into the vacuum of space, rocketing toward the sun.

"This is escort leader," Kai said. "My lads are in position. We'll escort the Sky Marshal out of Earth space."

"Acknowledged," I replied.

Kai was the leader of a five-Tomcat squadron that would make sure that no idiot did anything with the Sky Marshal's casket. They were to escort the Sky Marshal for the next fifteen hours, at which point, they would be relieved by Jenny on the *Piper*.

"And so ends the greatest military mind humans have ever known," the Sky Marshal said.

"Drinks are on me," I said. "We'll be over at the Spaceman's Asteroid tonight."

We traversed the halls back to the podium in the food court. Once we had all returned to our seats, Cestari stood up and the Chairman led her through the oath.

"I, Michaela Sasha Cestari, do solemnly swear that I will support and defend the Constitution of the Presidential Council against all enemies, foreign and domestic; that I will bear true faith and allegiance to the same; and that I take this obligation freely, without any mental reservation or purpose of evasion; and that I will well and faithfully discharge the duties and accept the responsibilities of the Sky Marshal of the Solar Military. I understand that the

Presidential Council is currently engaged in a declared war, and as such I have sole control of the Solar Military. I also understand that I bear all responsibility for everything done under my command during this war, and that once this war is over I will relinquish my command and will revert to my permanent rank. So help me God."

I was the first officer to stand, but soon every officer, or at least those not on the floating chairs, stood up and saluted our new commanding officer, Sky Marshal Michaela Sasha Cestari.

***

"To Sky Marshal Kitt," I said, raising my bottle of IBC root beer.

"To Sky Marshal Kitt," the other officers in the room echoed, raising their own glasses.

"And to our new Sky Marshal!" Jenny said. "Sky Marshal Cestari!"

"Oorah!" one of the marine officers yelled.

He got death stares from most of the Fleet and Force personnel.

"Anybody got funny stories about the Sky Marshal?" I asked.

"I don't think any of us could tell funny stories about Sky Marshal Kitt," Admiral Andrus responded. "As everybody said in their talks, he was brilliant at what he did, but that was all he did. I don't think he even played Triad."

"What?" Bronski said. "How is that possible?"

"Since you won the Army-Navy game, I'm sure that's hard for you to imagine," Sky Marshal Cestari said, "but nobody above O-4 has much time to play around."

"I don't know about that," Captain George McCloud spoke up. "My crew and officers always take time once a month to play a game of hurling in the mess deck. I always participate. It's good for crew morale."

"Interesting," Andrus said. "I've never seen a ship run like that."

"You've never been aboard the *Caledonia*," McCloud said with a grin.

"So, McCloud," I said. "How do you like your new rank?"

"Well, to be honest," McCloud said, "I preferred Colonel-Skipper, but once the Cabal was disbanded, I needed to join some branch of the military. I wanted to join the Force, even though the Cabal is working on getting all of its members into the Fleet. So, I called up Mr. Dalton. He wouldn't let me keep my title, but I prefer dress blacks to dress whites. And, anyway, white kilts look way too much like dresses."

We all laughed at that.

"I still think you guys look funny in kilts," I told him.

"I don't know," Lauren said. "I think they look cute. Maybe you should start wearing one."

"I've got to agree with Lauren on that," Kathy said, as she kissed George. "Men are hot in kilts."

"Maybe, but I wouldn't be caught dead in one!" I said, shaking my head and backing up into the bar. "Tom, when I give the high sign, I'm going to jump over the bar. You cover me, and I'll sneak out through the back."

"Nice try," Tom said. "I'd like to see you in a kilt, too."

"I was only joking," Lauren said. "McCloud was right, I don't think I want you wearing a white kilt."

"Anyway," I said. "What did you think about the way the news reported the Sky Marshal's death?"

"That was weak," Richard said. "But I'll help you out. I thought they did a good job. Though I did hear one station say that he committed suicide by not leaving the ship immediately."

"Civs." Jenny spat the word out like a swear word. "They just don't get it. The commander had to secure the ship before he could leave. It's only right and proper."

"I'll never understand civilian life, that's for sure," I said.

"Well," Jack said. "I don't think you'll have to. This war is going to last an awful long time. Chances are you'll buy the farm before you ever get a chance to retire."

"Thanks for the vote of confidence," Lauren said. "I'm kind of hoping we'll make it."

"You'll make it," Jack said. "It's Almek here who's always getting into trouble. He thought it was crazy for you to command a grapeshot frigate, but he's in harm's way much more than you are."

"Tell me about it," Lauren said, wrapping her arm around mine.

Marry her, I heard George McCloud whisper in my mind.

Get out of my head, I said, ending the link.

But I couldn't stop thinking about what he had said. The Sky Marshal had been someone I expected to outlive me. You just didn't think of him as being someone who would die. I was almost surprised he couldn't breathe hard vacuum just as well as air. But if the Sky Marshal could buy it, then so could I. Maybe McCloud was right.

***

"Good morning, spacers!" the Sky Marshal declared as she entered the room. We started to stand up and salute, but she waved us back into our seats. "We're all adults here, and by that I mean that we're all O-5 or above, so let's cut the saluting at these meetings, we've got too many things to work through to be slowed down by formalities.

"Okay, so we've got a couple key points to cover today. First, Jack's going to tell us about the state of the humans within the Alliance."

"Right," Jack said, standing up. "First off, the UME has finally been defeated! We know our victory wasn't cheap, but we outlasted them, and the human race is now united under one government … that is, excluding all members of Dalton Space Industries and of the Free Trader Coalition."

"Of course," Andrus whispered into my ear.

I just nodded and smiled.

"We lost quite a few ships in the Battles over Mars and Earth, but nothing compared to what we lost in the Battle for the Blockade or the Defense of Colony One. My people estimate that, at our current rate, the Alliance fleet will be stronger than it was before the Battle over Mars in just three month's time.

"On a happier note, before we defeated the UME, we had two out-of-system colonies, Branson and Lexington. Within three hours, three more colony ships will be sent out to recently explored systems. These systems are deeper into our own space, and further from the Draconians and the Garm. However, last night, we did send out a flotilla of ships, along with a couple constructors. These ships will build our first advanced military base. This base is placed closer to both the Passerines and the Draconians. Now that we no longer have to worry about the UME, our focus must now turn to the Draconians and the Garm. That is pretty much it. Things are looking good, at least for now."

Once Jack finished his report, the Sky Marshal adjourned the meeting. I was about to walk out, when she signaled for me to wait.

"Almek," she said, once the last person had left. "How do you like it on the *Starwarden*?"

"Why?" I asked, confused. "I love it, of course. There isn't anywhere I would rather be."

"Nowhere?" she prodded.

"Not that I can think of," I said, trying desperately to figure out where this was going.

"Almek," the Sky Marshal said, "you are now our most experienced human officer in the realm of inter-species relations."

"Okay," I said. "That's why I'm on the *Starwarden,* isn't it?"

"That's true, but how would you like to command the new outpost we're about to build on the border of Passerine and Draconian space, as a commodore."

"I wouldn't," I said, without hesitation. "I already tried my hand at commanding the orbitals over Branson. I'd rather be on something that moves, and I don't want to be a commodore. The real war is only just beginning, I don't want to be tied down on an outpost."

"Is there any way I could interest you?" she asked.

"No."

"The minute you leave the *Starwarden,* Jenny will be her captain. Your ship will be in good hands."

"You can order me to command the outpost," I said.

The Sky Marshal sighed. "You know I wouldn't do that. Think about it, though. You say the word, and you'll be there."

***

"You did say 'no,' right?" Lauren asked as soon as I'd finished telling her about my new job offer.

"Of course, I did," I responded. "I just wanted to let you know you about it."

"Thanks, Almek," she said, smiling at me. After a pause, she started up again. "I wish my cook was half the cook that yours is."

"Tell me about it," I said, as I dug into a delicious Passerine dish that Chefo had prepared for Lauren and me. "I don't know what I would do without Chefo."

"Thank you, sir," he said, as he entered carrying the next course.

"That wasn't meant for your ears," I said with a laugh.

"Forgive me, sir."

"So how's the squadron shaping out?" I asked Lauren, once Chefo had left.

"I'm training two new crews right now, but things are going well. I'm really excited to test out the enhancements to the EMP grapeshot generators that Richard has been working on. He said The Lab should have them ready to test in another month. If we have more powerful grapeshot, we'll wreak havoc on the Draconians. As it stands, their shields are very strong and our grapeshot is not. I sure hope Richard's new grapeshot lets us get through their shields."

"It would be nice," I said. "I just wish that we still had that galaxy drive. Imagine if we could travel between galaxies."

"That would be cool, but how would that help us? We already have enough enemies to contend with before we go and uncover new ones."

"True, but just imagine it. Traveling between galaxies. When I was a kid, I dreamed about traveling between the stars, but now the dreams can be bigger."

"There's too much space out there," Lauren said. "I'll stay here, thank you very much."

"So will I," I said. "I was only wishing."

Then my mind drifted, as it did so often, to the prospect of marrying Lauren. I was tempted to ask her right then and there, but I didn't have a ring.

"Lauren," I began.

"General quarters! General quarters! All personnel to battle stations! All personnel to battle stations! General quarters!"

###

If you would like to learn more about the author or
the Almek Manning series please visit the author's
webpage: http://www.almekmanning.com